Michael, What Page Are We On?

JACK CIOTTI

Copyright © 2018 Jack Ciotti

All rights reserved. No part(s) of this book may be repro-
duced, distributed or transmitted in any form, or by any
means, or stored in a database or retrieval systems without
prior expressed written permission of the author of this book.

ISBN: 978-1-5356-1436-8

Table of Contents

Chapter 1

Sister Says

I sat quietly in the catechism class, obediently following along in my small black prayer book as Sister Catherine, seated serenely at her desk, shapeless in her black habit and with the mantel of holiness resting heavily upon her shoulders, read aloud to us.

"Who made you?" she questioned.

Like the rushing of a small wind, the response from tiny throats automatically rolled back.

"God made us."

"Why did he make you?" she continued, shooting a piercing look at us to make sure everyone was paying rapt attention.

"To know him, to love him, to serve him in this world, and to be happy with him in the next," came the somewhat louder, if robotic, response. I wondered if everyone was as uncomfortable as me at the moment. Sister made us sit halfway on the seat to leave room for our guardian angel to sit next to us. Not daring to insult my angel, I let her have most of the chair in case she had a large rear end, so it took a constant balancing act not to fall on the floor. Disturbing the class could prove fatal.

Sister seemed pleased at our demure demeanor and continued with the reading. My mind became restless and I began to cast furtive glances around the room. There wasn't all that much of interest to see. The walls were unadorned except for a crucifix and clock above the blackboard in the front of the room and a calendar on the wall above my desk. Above the boxes with numbers and "feast days"- whatever they were - was a picture of a kitchen scene. It would have looked like my mother's kitchen, or my aunt's or grandmother's, except for the fact that this kitchen had an ugly green devil in it, complete with hooves, horns, wings, and a long tail. With a leering look on his face and a pointed red tongue hanging out, he was chasing a horrified little blond boy and girl around the kitchen table, trying to make them commit a sin. I was fascinated, though the irony of this picture in a Catholic school would be lost on me until far into adulthood.

Father Rocco, a middle-aged priest whose appearance fell within the range of priests at the time, being neither especially good-looking nor hideously repulsive, entered the room smiling, and

Sister signaled for us all to stand up. "Good afternoon, Father," we said in ragged unison.

"Good afternoon, children," he replied. "You may be seated." Then he began casually strolling up and down the aisles, pausing occasionally by one of our desks to rub the selected student's head or shoulders, saying he could feel angel wings or devil horns sprouting. It struck me as somewhat unfair that the girls seemed to be getting all the wings and the boys the horns. We all giggled, and even Sister smiled at these antics. Before departing, Father Rocco gave us a stern admonition.

"Remember, children, when you pass a Catholic church, you always make the sign of the cross," he said, demonstrating cross-making slowly for us, as if it were an extremely complicated process, almost beyond our comprehension. "And when you go by a church that isn't Catholic, you look the other way." He demonstrated this feat by turning his head swiftly to the right.

Satisfied that future angels and devils had learned their lesson on how to honor and snub churches of different faiths, he left the room and we returned to the reading of the little black catechism book. Sister looked up at the clock and noticed an hour had passed. Pointing to the clock, she smiled and said to her silent, and only slightly comprehending, audience, "Be thankful, children, you are now an hour closer to your death. And when you die, you will be with God." On that none-too-cheery note, we lined up, were duly dismissed, and emerged into the pleasant sunshine and still-living world outside.

Catechism classes during the late 1950s in New York took place on Wednesday afternoons. The public school would dismiss at noon and the Catholic kids would be sent, unescorted, to St. Whoever's, which, in my case, was St. Perpetua's, two blocks down the street. As this was an Italian neighborhood populated with many *mamadellas* in their perpetual funeral black and old men in sweater vests, bow ties, and fedoras, safety was not an issue. Perfect protectors, they watched you closely, ready to pounce on any act of misbehavior and report it to your parents. Midway between schools we were met by a tsunami of screaming Catholic school kids in blue uniforms heading home, the boys ripping off their ties as they raced by. They didn't look like they cared if even a bishop was watching. Their wild behavior was explained to me by my mother, who said that they were so strictly disciplined during the day that they were just releasing all their pent-up energy. So, every Wednesday I watched, amazed, at the melee of pleated plaid skirts and loud boys as the dark blue wave crested over us.

As the catechism kids got older and began preparing for communions and confirmations, we got a taste of some of that discipline. If you were stupid enough to cut up in class, the infamous ruler on the knuckles was the norm. One overactive friend of mine contained in a Catholic school had so many rulers broken over his knuckles, the priest sent his father a bill for reimbursement. But there were other forms of torture, and each Sister seemed to have their personal favorite. Boys were smacked in the back of the head for misbehaving, and the girls who were not paying attention had their long hair pulled. If you spoke, you had to kneel in the aisle with your hands in a praying position for the entire class. Less harmful physically, but with longer-lasting mental damage, was the Catholic guilt trip and the injected fear of God - and the Communists.

"The Communists are coming," was the serious-faced Father Peter's dire prediction to our class of scared nine-year-old, Davy Crockett-inspired patriots. "They hate Jesus. When they get here, the Communist soldiers will go to the church, dump the hosts in the street, and step on them!" he continued, stomping his right foot to give more impact to his words. "It's up to you children to run to the church first and eat the hosts before the Communists can get them," he commanded. Satisfied that the hosts would now be safe due to the heroism of young crusaders, he headed for the classroom door. Then he turned, smiling at the still stunned students, and tossed in an afterthought.

"Oh, and by the way, be sure to remind your parents that there is a second collection for the bishop's fund this Sunday at Mass."

I had no idea what a Communist was but, with Father Peter's scary description of them embedded in my mind, I envisioned them like Godzilla and other monsters from Japanese horror films that had me hiding behind the seat in sheer terror at the movie theater. I figured I would probably be incinerated by fiery monster breath before I could gobble up all the hosts, so I was shocked to see some normal-looking young people on the cover of a *Life* magazine a few weeks later under the heading "The Future of Communism." To my vast relief, they didn't appear very threatening, though they looked athletic and could probably outrun me to the church. But if I got there first and rescued the hosts from the hungry Russians, would I go straight to heaven for my heroics when the Communist soldiers killed me? It all seemed so confusing to a child, and adulthood didn't offer any easier explanations.

To make matters worse, Sister introduced another life-threatening force to us: venial sins. She explained that they weren't as bad as mortal sins, but if you didn't confess every Sunday and do a proper penance for them, they left marks on your soul that quickly added up. To illustrate this point, she went to the board and drew a circle.

"This is your soul," she said sternly, pointing to her somewhat lopsided creation, "and these are venial sins." She made scattered X's inside the circle. "Going to confession makes them go away," she explained, erasing the X's. "But if you don't get rid of them, they eventually turn your soul black, and that could have very bad consequences," she warned, her frowning face emphasizing the fact. "I'm doomed," I thought hopelessly. "My soul will fill up with venial sins, turn black, and I'll drop dead before I can get to confession. If the Communists don't do me in, the venial sins will."

Having been told at home that the nuns were "God's angels on earth," I had blind faith in everything that they told me. The Sisters' appearance alone screamed authority. Clad in their more-than-modest habits as they were, I had no conception that they even had normal human bodies. All that I ever saw were the flawless complexions of their faces, which they achieved, I was informed by a friend, by washing only with holy water.

To rid myself of those life-threatening venial sins, I went without fail to confession every Saturday afternoon and communion every Sunday. I said the same tired and trite confession of sins every time. "I lied to my parents two times and teased my baby sister three times." You had to remember the exact amount of times you did these awful things. It would have been great to have had some really impressive mortal sins, the ones reserved mostly for adults, like larceny, murder, or adultery (whatever that was), just to hear the reaction of the priest, but I had to make do with the insipid childhood variety.

When my sister and I went to Mass by ourselves, we were relegated to the "Children's Section," with a glowering nun chaperoning over us like a black-cloaked Cerberus.

Not even the slightest breach of decorum seemed to get past her. If you talked, giggled, or neglected the responses, a reproving look was quickly riveted on you. My attention wandered and my eyes would scan the paintings and reliefs on the walls for distraction. I thought Mary was pretty, and the Roman soldiers looked really cool with their red capes, helmets, and spears. The saints, however, looked hideous with their bare feet, bald heads, and long beards, so I assumed that a prerequisite for sainthood was unusual ugliness.

As we dutifully filed out of the church when the Mass was finished, the children had to pass the Sister standing next to the holy water and, for some, face the moment of truth. If you had done nothing wrong, you had nothing to fear and received a brief nod as you breezed by. But woe to those who had misbehaved.

"I saw you giggling during Mass," Sister said, glaring at two suddenly terrified girls. "Do you know you made the Virgin Mary cry? She's crying right now, and it's your fault," she continued accusingly, and the guilty girls would invariably tear up. The Mary guilt trip didn't work well with the boys, so they usually got a slap on the back of the head instead.

"Hand it over," Sister demanded with an outstretched hand to anyone she spotted not contributing a coin to the basket collection. "I know you're going to buy candy at the store on your way home instead of giving God his gift."

She would then fix an accusing eye on the guilty party, and the shame-faced thief would slowly produce the quarter from his or her pocket. Actually, we enjoyed the excitement of these Sunday dramas, just as long as Sister's anger wasn't directed at us.

A source of endless entertainment was the "League of Decency" list in the church foyer, advising parishioners what, as good Catholics, we could and could not watch. Any movie that starred Elizabeth Taylor, Marilyn Monroe, or Brigitte Bardot was forbidden fruit. I surmised that those actresses must be similar to the sinister bad women in the Bible that fascinated me, like Jezebel, Delilah, and Salome. Of course, these were the films the kids wanted to see, though we didn't really know why, except that they held the titillating element of the wicked and the forbidden.

Symbols of the faith could be seen throughout our neighborhood. It seemed that every other house had a serene Mary on the Half-shell cement ornament in the front yard, usually standing next to a whimsical donkey and cart. There was a direct connection because the donkey carried Mary to Bethlehem, and that's why, to this day, the donkey has a cross on its back (or so I was informed). No Italian grandmother's bedroom was complete without a Madonna picture on the wall, usually with withered palms from the last Palm Sunday half-wedged behind it. And the manger scene, be it of plaster or plastic, was proudly displayed in many front yards during the Christmas season. Some lucky family member would sneak out on cold Christmas Eves, after consuming the requisite seven fish, to place the baby Jesus in his crib.

All of this may seem silly, if not slightly bizarre, yet it was singularly comforting to a child. Conformity and rituals do serve a purpose. God was in his heaven and, if you were good, one day you would be there, too. It was that simple. Although some things, like limbo, I never really understood. Babies, we were told, couldn't go to heaven if they died before they were baptized. They spent an eternity in limbo. The only limbo I knew was the dance where you bent backwards under a lowered stick while Chubby Checker sang "Limbo Rock." I couldn't picture babies having to do the limbo forever when they never did anything to annoy anyone except cry and need their diapers changed.

Hell, with its fire and pitchforks, was horrifying, but purgatory didn't exactly seem like a day at the beach either. You suffered there, too. Purgatory always seemed to me like being in jail, and, if enough people prayed and did good deeds for you, you got out on parole and into heaven. But what if no one wanted to help you out? How did anyone even know you were there? It seemed easier to just get the whole confusing mess over with and go straight to hell.

As I moved into my teenage years, religion began to seem more like a bargaining process: you promised God good behavior in return for favors. But both God and I broke our sides of the bargain time and again.

My friends and I could at times be irreverent. One brought a joke to our school cafeteria lunch table that we thought was hilarious. At the end of the day, some of us went to the school library where, for a dime, you could make your own copy on the Xerox machine. The joke, called "THE DONKEY", went something like this:

THE DONKEY

Father Murphy was a priest in a very poor parish and asked for suggestions on how to raise money for the church. One of the parishioners mentioned that all horse owners had money, so Father Murphy went to an auction and bought a horse. As it turned out, the horse was a donkey. He decided to enter the donkey in a race anyway and it finished third. The next day, the sports page headline read: "Father Murphy's Ass Shows."

The archbishop saw the headline and was very displeased.

The next day, the donkey came in first, and the headline read: "Father Murphy's Ass Out in Front." The next day, the donkey finished second, and the headline read: "Father Murphy's Ass Back in Place."

The archbishop was up in arms and forbade the priest from entering the donkey in any more races. The headline then read: "Archbishop Scratches Father Murphy's Ass."

In desperation, the archbishop ordered Father Murphy to dispose of the animal. He was unable to sell it, so he gave it to Sister Agatha, who sold the donkey for $10,000. The headline the next day read: "Sister Agatha Peddles Her Ass for $10,000."

They buried the archbishop three days later.

I continued to attend Mass, fearing the consequences if I didn't, and ardently wished I could be as devout as my grandmother. Every Sunday, without fail, she somehow squeezed her 200-pound body into a girdle, struggled into a Lane Bryant dress, and headed for Mass. Hoping to get some extra consideration on the Day of Judgement, she even purchased an expensive marble baptismal font for the church of her choice.

Her faith and generosity were rewarded in a strange way before she even passed on. One day, she was driving on Interstate 95 from her winter retirement home in Florida when her car got a flat tire in a swampy area of South Carolina. Understandably scared, she prayed for assistance to come from a passing motorist or policeman. According to her, what she received instead was divine intervention. Dressed all in white, Jesus appeared between two moss-hung cypress trees, strolled silently to her car, and expertly changed the flat. Then he silently vanished back into the swamp.

I took her Jesus sighting story in stride, not wanting to experience the repercussions of questioning it. I figured if Jesus could turn water into wine and multiply fish and loaves, he could certainly change a flat tire. But I noticed she did get AAA soon after, probably figuring even someone as devote as herself didn't rate a repeat miracle. A diagnosis of dementia was rendered a decade later.

Finally, in my eighteenth year, temptation trumped fear. I skipped Mass and spent a sun-splashed, fun-filled day at the beach. When I didn't drown or get devoured by sharks, it was all over. Except for weddings and funerals, I didn't set foot in a church again. All that remained of a once active Catholic conscience was an occasional sense of guilt that could usually be quickly quenched. Religion, except for a quick bedtime prayer, was now in the rearview mirror, and it would remain there for decades.

Chapter 2

Praise the Lord and Pass the Amunition

Time went by and life could be measured by different dances done, various hairstyles worn, different cars driven, and assorted jobs and bosses. Throughout the years, I never relinquished the love I had acquired during childhood for history and literature. When I attended college, I majored in both subjects. One day, I saw an ad for a Civil War reenactment in the area and decided to attend, not knowing that this small decision would begin a strange chain of events that would culminate in a career as, of all the improbable things, a Catholic school teacher.

The reenactment was a wonderful scenario, complete with camps, people in period dress, and a realistic looking battle. As a kid, my friends and I played soldiers in the backyard, wearing cardboard kepis, shooting each other with harmless toy guns, and having an all-around great time imitating the bloodless, over-the-top death scenes we watched on early TV shows. In some ways, the reenactment was the same thing, only on a higher level, and the little boy in me wanted to be a part of it.

I signed up with a reenacting unit; purchased a rifle, uniform, and tent; and began re-fighting the Civil War. The tent was a mere formality as I had no intention of ever spending the night in it, my camping days being behind me. I wanted the comfort of a "cement tent," also known as the nearest motel. I thought sleeping in the tent was required, so at my first reenactment I resorted to subterfuge. When night fell and the eating, drinking, and singing around the campfire died down, I pretended to yawn. After wishing everyone a good night, I went into my tent and tied the flaps. Ten minutes later, I slipped out the back with savage stealth and took off for the motel. There I showered and shaved and got a great night's rest.

At five the next morning, I went back into the cold and damp camp and snuck into my tent the same way I had exited. The version of an alarm clock in camp was a cannon fired at seven A.M. I emerged from the tent clean, refreshed, and groomed, and joined the tired, disheveled, and grumpy group. They stared at me in amazement but, fortunately, asked no questions. This charade proved to be too much trouble though, so I gave it up and just went to a motel from then on and (surprise!) no one cared.

Reenacting proved to be a great learning experience and provided me with more knowledge about what life was like before modern conveniences than reading a hundred books could have accomplished. It was uncomfortable at best and, when it came to the port-o-sans, it literally stunk. I was also made aware of why they took men into the service in their teens, not their forties. But, despite the heat, cold, bugs, and mud, it was fun.

The most pleasing element of reenacting was performing scenarios for the people who came to watch us, though at times my friends and I forgot our age and played childish pranks on each other. When a female reenactor was portraying an army laundress cleaning period clothing, we secretly slipped a pair of black Calvin Kline jockey shorts into her washtub. She removed the clothing piece by piece and wrung it out, explained what it was, and hung it on a line in front of her assembled audience. When she lifted the underwear out of the tub, she screamed while the onlookers laughed. Spotting me, and surmising that I was the culprit, she flung the wet underwear at my face.

Another scenario where we had some fun was at Miss Annie's funeral. Sutlers are people who sell Civil War products at the reenactments and generally have some novelty items available, as well. One such item was a token from a Civil War era whorehouse. It had the name of the establishment, "Fat Sue's," engraved on one side and the amount of good times it brought on the other. Miss Annie was laid out in a period correct coffin while the reenactors and spectators filed past to pay their last respects. When it was my turn to mourn Miss Annie, I placed the coins over her closed eyes. She didn't move because she thought it was part of the production. Plus, she was supposed to be dead. When those behind me got their turn to view the corpse, they were treated to the sight of the tokens on Miss Annie's eyes saying, "GOOD FOR ONE SCREW." It took me some time to get back into Miss Annie's good graces.

Another feature of reenacting was the elegant balls that we attended. I did better on the firing line than the dance floor. The first one I attended had a dinner first, and I was seated across from a lady that I liked. We all had dance cards to fill out to claim a certain dance with the lady of our choice. Miss Henny handed me her card across the table to reserve the Grand March, the first dance of the evening, with her. I signed my name and, while passing the card back to her, put it too close to a candle, where it instantly caught on fire. My first impulse was to blow it out, but I blew the flame onto Miss Henny's dress. She screamed and, thinking quickly, beat the fire out with a napkin.

Needless to say, I didn't get Miss Henny as a dancing partner, which proved fortunate for her. While turning in a waltz step with another lady, I accidentally stomped on her foot with my boot. Her slipper came off as she yelped and, with my next graceful step, I kicked her detached footwear clear across the dance floor and under an occupied table. Playing the gentleman, I retrieved it for her as she hobbled off the dance floor, sank onto an empty chair, and fumbled with her flounces and hoop skirt to find and massage her injured foot. Everyone in attendance viewed these antics, so females for the remainder of the evening bypassed me and I was relegated to a male version of a wallflower. From then on, I avoided the balls and only participated in the battles where, even armed with a weapon, I proved less deadly.

Being a Civil War and, eventually, Revolutionary War reenactor soon led to playing the part of a soldier in movies and documentaries. It may sound great, but there is no glamour, or money, in being an extra. The payoff is spotting your split-second moment on the screen. To achieve this thrill meant traveling to one gas station towns hidden in the back of beyond, standing in a freezing or scorched field from sunrise to sunset, waiting for hours while the battle scenes are set up all the while not daring to sit down for fear red ants will sting you, and doing the same take over and over again. The pay for all this fun ranged from a princely $150 dollars per day and delicious meals down to not a cent and having to buy your own lunch from a crummy roach coach. The producers of these films were no fools. They knew that, being reenactors and loving history, we would put up with all this inconvenience for the happiness of appearing in a historical drama.

Some moments on these sets were memorable, for reasons both good and bad. During the filming of *Gettysburg*, while filling my canteen at a water truck, I had the honor of making the acquaintance of two colorful characters from the mountains of western North Carolina who went by the names of Coondick and Pappy. Coondick was sort of slow and would roll his eyes searching for the right words to form a sentence in response to a simple question. When I asked him about the origin of his nickname - and I hoped it was his nickname - he proudly pointed to a curved bone stuck into his slouch hat.

"I killed a raccoon," he explained in a halting twang. "The coon is the only animal with a bone in its dick, and as I always wear it in my hat, my friends named me Coondick." That answered my question and provided me with an animal anatomy lesson. How Pappy got his nickname was evident by the shoulder length white hair and foot-long beard that framed his seamed and weather- beaten face. They seemed neighborly enough, so when they offered me a swig of their homemade moonshine, I said, "Sure."

We were soon seated together on a nearby bale of hay. Pappy produced a mason jar of what looked like water but he said was white lightning. He unscrewed and lifted the lid. Then, with a smile showing some missing front teeth, he passed the jar to me. I took a large gulp, but the burning liquid didn't seem to travel to my stomach, making a beeline for my brain instead. My head felt like it was about to explode and, dazed, I steadied myself on the hay and handed it back. Both seemed to enjoy my response to their joy juice immensely, and Pappy, seeming bent on making me even sicker, pulled a large twist of tobacco from his pocket and offered me a "chaw." Not wanting to be rude, and having smoked cigarettes in the past, I bit off a large piece and began chewing. My face screwed up and my head shook as it tasted like someone had walked into my mouth and died. Years earlier, my friend had been caught smoking a cigarette in the high school and the teacher made him eat it in front of the class. Now I knew just how he felt!

Feeling it was time to "git while the gittin' was good," I thanked them for their southern hospitality and staggered off, heading for the nearest toothbrush, toothpaste, and bottle of painkillers.

The set of a prominent Revolutionary War movie presented its own problems. During a major battle scene, the director sent the Loyalist cavalry charging across the same spot on a smoke-filled field already occupied with our advancing British battle line. I came within feet of being ridden down by a saber-swinging trooper, and the reenactor next to me had his foot trod on by a horse. An ambulance came and hauled him away with little ceremony, and the director appeared aggravated that the scene had to be redone. I hope the mangled reenactor received a good settlement.

At one point we spotted the star of the film and, because we were the British and he was the American hero, we good-naturedly heckled him. His response was mooning us. We saw more of his anatomy than we had expected, or wanted, to see.

Arguably, my most embarrassing reenacting moment occurred at a local event. The British unit I was a member of wore bearskin helmets. During the fiercest part of a battle, while firing my musket, some sparks flew up from the flash pan and ignited the fur of the bearskin, causing it to smolder and smoke like a hairy chimney. Hundreds of spectators burst into loud laughter, while I, unaware of what was happening on my head, continued to snarl and yell "huzzah" at the American enemies. Finally, a friend next to me in our line spotted the source of the crowd's amusement, and, though laughing himself silly at the ludicrous sight, knocked the now bizarre bearskin off my head with his musket. Then both of us began stomping on the overheated headgear. Totally humiliated, I feigned being shot, fell to the ground, and buried my face in the concealing grass until the battle was over.

About this time, a friend's sister, Rosemary Roberts, found out that I was involved in these interesting historical scenarios and asked if I would visit her fifth-grade class in my uniform and talk about the Civil War. Rosemary had once desired to be a nun, but before her final vows, she exchanged her habit for a bikini and white boots and became a cage-enclosed go-go dancer in a bar on the Jersey Shore.

The visit to her class turned out to be fun and the students really enjoyed it. This led to many other historical presentations at numerous schools in the area. Of course, the kids loved these presentations as it meant they got out of class for over an hour and were entertained. I thought the students were wonderful because I didn't have to worry about the mundane tasks like discipline and getting them to pass tests or turn in homework.

As if in a logical, if somewhat strange, progression, the school presentations led to the making of an award-winning educational video. At a town historical society meeting, I met a friend's wife, Karen. Karen assisted in some direct-to-video movie productions and was interested in my school presentations. She came with me to watch my next presentation, liked what she saw, and told me that she would broach the topic of making an educational video to her producer friend, Peter.

I met with the two of them at the local Pizza Hut- hardly a Hollywood hangout- and a handshake deal was done. I was highly impressed with their impeccable credentials to make a children's video. The last film Karen was involved in was a production in which a man rebuilds his dead girlfriend with body parts collected from the hookers he murders. She showed me the button from the recent premiere which portrayed a pieced-hooker and said, "Hey, big boy" when the back was pressed.

As the producer of my video, Peter's claim to fame was that he had directed Zsa Zsa Gabor in a commercial, so I knew I was in the hands of someone associated with top talent.

The production took place on Peter's woodsy property in a rural area. Battle and camp scenes had already been filmed at a reenactment and would be cut in to look as if we were there. Some of my friend's kids were in the video, along with my cousin, who was cast as the Southern Belle. The soundman was to bring his kids, as well. Peter's teenage son was provided by nepotism with the role of the Yankee soldier, and an attractive girl in film school was there to help on the set.

Everything seemed perfect, yet by the end of the shoot we were proof that Murphy's Law - anything that can go wrong, will - was more than an adage.

The day of the filming was ninety-five degrees with humidity to match. I was the first to arrive at Peter's house, which was hidden at the end of a long, twisting road and hard to locate. Then Karen arrived with her husband, who was fascinated with my rifle and asked to hold it. When I handed it over, he yanked the trigger back too quickly and broke the spring. So much for my firing demonstration in the video.

The filming was supposed to begin at nine. Everyone was there and set to go except the soundman and his kids. So, we waited. And waited! Finally, at ten, a sweating and panting Paulo strolled into the backyard with his two tired kids in tow. They had gotten a ride up from the Bronx and when Paulo saw the correct street sign, he told the driver to let them out, forgetting that the grid pattern of the city didn't exist up in the woods and that Peter's house was still a hot, uphill mile away.

Paulo's two kids hadn't had breakfast and were justifiably hungry and cranky. While they were being served some food, Michael, Peter's son, who should have been learning his lines, took a shine to the girl from film school and started desperately flirting with her, trying to set up a future date before his girlfriend, who was due to visit that afternoon, made her now undesired appearance.

The filming finally started in the stifling heat. Every time I touched a metal object to show and describe to the kids, my fingers flamed. My cousin, who was hidden in the woods awaiting her cue, kept crying out as she constantly shook off assorted species of bugs that crawled all over her hoop-skirted dress. Michael wasted his time with the film school girl, who stupidly stepped into a gopher hole, twisted her ankle, and was hauled off to an emergency room. When the time arrived for his simple part, he kept flubbing his lines. The kids, who were supposed to appear wildly enthusiastic whenever I showed them an artifact, increasingly looked bored to death. Then, to add to the fun, Peter took out his mounting frustration with the production by throwing a camera battery at Karen and came close to getting clobbered by her husband.

With all these various disasters, I figured the video was doomed. Yet, by some miracle and exceedingly good editing, the educational film somehow went on to win the Parent's Choice Award that year, which looked wonderful on a resume.

Chapter 3

And He's Safe in the Fold Once More

When the company I worked for offered us an early buyout, I leaped at the opportunity. Figuring it was either now or never, I decided that it was time to teach. I would find out the hard way that entertaining students at random engagements spread throughout the year and being in a classroom with them every day are two entirely different things, requiring another range of talents entirely.

I decided to apply to Catholic schools because, at the time, you could get a teaching position there without having state certification. I paid twenty dollars to be placed on a list of Catholic schools that were looking for teachers for the coming school year. Within three weeks I had four interviews. Having not been on an interview in decades, I was somewhat apprehensive, not knowing exactly what to expect. My fears proved to be unfounded as the principals were all pleasant enough, yet the situations in each of the schools were very different.

My first interview was at a school in a suburb of New York City where the principal was a priest. He greeted me cordially, presented me with a standard job form to fill out, and led me to a table in the library to proceed with the writing while he went about his business back in his office. I was making headway until I came to a word I had to use but couldn't spell. As I was alone in the library, I began to softly sound out the word but, after writing it down, it just didn't look right. Now what? Deliverance came when I spotted a large dictionary on the shelf in front of me.

While writing down the correct spelling, I heard footsteps and, looking up, saw the priest coming down the hall toward the library. *Oh my God, Father is coming!* Forty years of adult life quickly faded, and I felt like a little boy about to be caught cheating by a frightening authority figure. Without thinking, I flung the dictionary down on my lap, causing great pain to a sensitive area, and pushed my chair under the table.

"Are you almost finished?" he questioned. I was almost finished all right, as I could barely talk.

"I'll be done in a moment," I managed to whisper, smiling weakly.

"I'll be in my office," he said, eying me suspiciously before turning and walking away. With a sigh of relief, I sat there and slowly recovered. Then

I returned the dictionary to the shelf and brought the employment form to the priest. After exchanging some pleasantries, he promised to get back to me. I'm glad I didn't hold my breath waiting as I never did hear back, nor will anyone else anymore as that school is now shuttered.

The next interview was, in a sense, an improvement. At least I didn't leave physically injured, just mentally depressed. The school was in an area that had deteriorated over the years. Let's just say I wouldn't want to be there after dark. In fact, I was nervous being there in broad daylight. You could tell that the church-convent-school complex must have been the pride of the neighborhood at one time, the center of religious and cultural activities. What remained was a run-down building that looked unloved. I went to the front door and rang the buzzer.

"And who might it be?" called an older female voice with an Irish brogue so thick you could cut it with a knife.

"I'm Mr. Consorte and I have an appointment with Mrs. Horan."

"I'll be right down to let you in," she promised. About sixty seconds later, the heavy door was pulled open to reveal a slim, severely out-of-breath woman in her seventies with a warm smile. She was to be one of the few cheery memories of this dreary mausoleum masquerading as a school.

"I'm Peggy. Just follow me," she said sprightly as she led me up an old and worn staircase to the second floor, down a long hallway crying for a coat of fresh paint, and into an antiquated office that appeared to be furnished and decorated from the cast offs of a cheap yard sale from another era. It looked as if nothing had been replaced or updated in the school since 1960. I felt like Pip in *Great Expectations* waiting for Miss Havisham to suddenly stroll by in a tattered wedding gown.

"Do you have to do this every time someone comes to the door?" I asked, amazed that she managed the heart attack-inducing climb from door to office without the outward appearance of strain.

"Oh yes, it keeps me young and thin," she joked. "But it does get harder to do every year." I'm sure it did.

Peggy handed me the now familiar employment form to fill out while Mrs. Horan was screaming at someone from behind her closed principal's office door. Both she and I were done at the same time. Her door opened to reveal a smirking male student who appeared to be about thirteen. As he left the office, she screamed a parting shot.

"And you better not cause Miss Bartoe to send you down here again!" Then the gray haired, tough little munchkin of a woman turned to me. "You know, ninety percent of the students are good, and then there's the other ten percent," she said, jabbing her thumb in the direction of the departed student. Despite her diminutive height and age, she seemed to be strong-minded. I guessed that she had to be to survive there.

"If I give you this job, just promise you won't leave after a year," she said when we were seated in her office. "Many times, I've spent the year training new teachers and then they leave."

Gee, I couldn't guess why. The entire place seemed to be a sad ghost of what it once was, and, with the picture of this gloomy scene of dreary decay in my mind, I shivered as I drove away.

About two weeks later, a call came from Mrs. Horan. Between her screams at a student, who was obviously in her office for some offense, she delivered a job offer, which I declined with good reason. I already had another job at a school that, on the surface, appeared to be adorable.

Another interview materialized within a week in the city of Braadvet. The neighborhood wasn't the best, but the school seemed nice enough. The principal, Mr. Thomas, was a boyish looking man in his thirties. When he read my references, a smile spread over his face.

"You list here as a reference Rosemary Roberts. If it's the same person, she was my mentor when I began teaching. She was so helpful to me, and we had a great time together," he beamed. When we compared notes about Rosemary, we realized she was one and the same person. This strange coincidence sealed the deal. He called Rosemary that evening, chatted for a happy hour and a half with her, and got back to me the next day.

"I want to hire you, but I have to go by protocol and call some other people first on the hiring list. So, I'll do that and get back to you."

"Thanks," I said. "I actually have another interview set up for tomorrow. I already told the principal that I would be there, so I'd better go."

Some things in life can't be explained by rational means, and certain situations are almost spooky. This is how it was with the next school, Our Lady of the Holy Rosary Beads. I had driven past it on my way to work at my telecommunications consulting job for the past two years and had a strange feeling each time I went by that I would somehow be in there one day. It was in a nice neighborhood, and, fronted by banks of flowers, looked serene and adorable. This place seemed to be the answer to a prospective teacher's dream, and I entered the interview with high hopes.

The principal, Mrs. Devilica, didn't exactly leave me falling by the roadside at her beauty. To put it bluntly, her body bore a close resemblance to the Emily Elephant Weeble, and her complexion looked as though she had barbed wire in her makeup. For the crowning glory, her Buster Brown styled hair was inked black, which, I was to soon discover, perfectly matched the hue of her heart. But I was here for a job, not a date, and she seemed very businesslike, asked all the pertinent questions, and appeared satisfied with my answers.

"You seem to have a lot to offer the students. I just want to see you teach a lesson before I offer you a contract. Can you be here at ten tomorrow?" she asked.

"I certainly can," I replied, smiling. I left the school and sped home with a happy heart.

At ten the next morning, I followed a waddling Mrs. Devilica into a classroom on the second floor and faced a group of fresh-faced and attentive students, all sitting with their placid hands folded in front of them atop their desks. She introduced me and then squeezed herself into a seat behind a desk in the back of the room. I taught a lesson on the Civil War, passed around plenty of articles for the students to see, and answered all their questions as Mrs. Devilica watched with an inscrutable expression. I didn't know if she was pleased or repulsed until we returned to her office.

"That was fine," she said. "You'll be teaching sixth, seventh, and eighth-grade Social Studies and Religion. Do you want the job?"

"Of course," I replied, beaming.

"You are a practicing Catholic, aren't you?" she asked.

Yes," I lied stoutly.

"Good. Father Benzitti likes the teachers to be practicing Catholics."

After signing the contract, she gave me the books from the courses I would be teaching to study over the summer.

I left her with an impulsive parting remark: "I'll make sure that you never have any reason to regret your decision." And I meant that statement from the bottom of my heart, not realizing how ironic it would be in the near future.

The first thing I did when I arrived home was to phone my mother. "As a kid, you always told me that if I was bad I was going to be put in a Catholic school," I told her. "Well, I must have been an awful adult, because your threat came true." Then I realized that not having been to Mass in thirty years might present a slight problem if I was to teach Religion. They could be saying the Mass in Mongolian for all I knew. The last time I spoke directly to a priest in a church setting was when I was twenty-one and an usher in a friend's wedding. The groom had the male members of the wedding party over to his house before the ceremony for a few drinks. In my case, it was a few too many. When we got to the church and the father of the bride and the priest saw the condition I was in, they pulled me into a side chapel and, their eyes wide with rage, barked that they would break my damn neck if I messed up the wedding. Not exactly a benediction, and, with my life on the line, I sobered up fast.

The best way to familiarize myself with a Mass was, of course, to attend one. The very next morning found me going to eight o'clock Mass at the little church in my town's Italian neighborhood. The sparse crowd consisted mostly of ancient women in black, probably there to pray for long-dead husbands, and a spattering of middle-aged ex-drug addicts who had somehow reformed and found Jesus. Despite their long, gray ponytails and tired faces, I still recognized some as fellow classmates from a faraway past.

My payback for not going to church for eons was unknowingly picking the day when they do the Rosary. It seemed interminable. Fortunately, the Mass was pretty much as I remembered it, except that they had replaced Holy Ghost with Holy Spirit. I was on the way to my religious revival.

After studying from the teacher's editions of the textbooks during the summer, I thought that I was well prepared for my first day. Then came three days of new teacher orientation classes in the cafeteria of a local Catholic high school. The place was packed, mostly with women just out of college and a few young men. At any Catholic teacher conference in the years to come you could always count the men on your ten fingers. Because I had been in the business world for decades, I had dressed conservatively for the conference. The younger new hires looked and behaved like they were on their way to the beach, and I half expected to have to duck a flying Frisbee. Remembering the term "generation gap" from my youth, I sadly realized that I was now on the other side of it.

The fat, jolly, somewhat effeminate man in charge, Mr. Marsala, was an ex-principal who had moved on to a probably easier position. His opening line was, "I know that most of you are here because you couldn't get jobs in the public schools." He was joking, yet many a truth is said in jest, and we knew in the present case it was all too true. The wide disparity in salary and benefits between public and private schools meant that, in most cases, the fresh faces before him were there due to default.

The would-be teachers talked loudly amongst themselves while Mr. Marsala attempted to lecture and, in general, they gave him little respect. I found this strange since, at the moment, he was their big boss, and I realized I was definitely from a more mannered, bygone generation.

"Be quiet!" he finally bellowed with a frown. Shocked into silence, they shut up. Then ancient Sister Jean went to the microphone to tell teaching tales from the beginning of her career, which, judging from her appearance, could have been the year of the flood.

"My first class had forty-five students in it," she said, and her audience gasped in horror. "People told me I was too pretty to be a nun, but I was infused with love for Jesus," she informed us with glowing eyes. She summed up discipline hints with the admonition, "Don't smile until Christmas."

The orientation was actually enjoyable as everyone seemed excited in anticipation of their first teaching job. Well, almost everyone. One good-looking young man sat quiet and morose at our table. He skipped out at lunchtime on the second day and didn't return for the afternoon session, probably thinking that, with so many people there, Mr. Marsala wouldn't notice. But, for some reason, he did. The young man was reprimanded the next morning. This incident seemed trivial at the time, yet the behavior of these two strangers would play a key role in my life within a year.

At the end of the last day, Mr. Marsala gave us advice on how to behave. "Don't touch the students," he warned, waving a finger at us like a reproving grandmother. "And always be careful where you are seen and how you are dressed." With a "good luck and God bless," he turned away from us and pompously paraded out the door. Then the teachers stampeded

for the exits to beat the snarl of traffic leaving the
parking lot.

Chapter 4

Across the River Styx

I pulled into the parking lot of Our Lady of The Holy Rosary Beads with some trepidation the next day. There were only two days left before the beginning of the school year. Things that didn't seem important months ago were now a major concern since the day of reckoning had finally come. Did I really know what I was doing? Even more important, would the students believe I knew what I was doing? Would they like me? Could I get them to do well? Could I not use a bathroom for hours at a time without bursting my bladder?

Remembering all too well the empty walls of the classrooms of my childhood, I had purchased posters of the different time periods I would be teaching and began putting them up. A friend had provided me with reproductions of ancient Egyptian artwork when she found out I would be teaching that time period, and I was arranging them on a wall when the sixth grade homeroom teacher walked in, distracting me.

"I'm Marlene, the science and math teacher," she said, unsmiling, as an introduction. Marlene appeared to be in her mid-thirties and of more than ample proportions. The yoke of some sorrow seemed to weigh her down as her eyes stared directly and uncompromisingly at me. After we exchanged the usual background information, she confided that she had been an overweight child and the other kids made fun of her during her school days.

While making the proper, sympathetic responses, all I could think was, "What the hell kind of a greeting is this? 'Hi, how are you? I had a miserable childhood.'" If first impressions can be trusted, she didn't seem like she would be much fun to work with, and she wasn't.

The next day was a teachers' meeting and, as it was the first one of the year, it began with a Mass. For the rest of the monthly meetings, a quick prayer would serve to get the show on the road. A quick glance around the room revealed women ranging in age from their early twenties to their fifties in assorted sizes and shapes. Sister Veronica, an older nun dressed in a habit, sat quietly in the front, a place of honor. She was the sole survivor from the attached convent who was still capable of teaching. The rest had long since been relegated to the Mother Home, where they would await their judgment day and be rewarded for their decades of selfless work. Her classroom was the first one down the hall from the convent door and, when winter came, I envied her commute.

The agenda for the school year was laid out and all questions were asked and answered by the dour Mrs. Devilica. But when the hot trays of catered food were brought in, she suddenly perked up and swiftly concluded the meeting. The teachers lined up at the food table and, bred to gentlemanly conduct, I let all the ladies go first. That proved to be a mistake as most of them tanked up on the baked ziti and left me the hard scrapings I could barely dislodge from the sides of the tray. This exhibition of one of the seven deadly sins led to a silent vow never to be last in line again.

When the feeding frenzy ended, we went to our classrooms to finish decorating and setting up for the first day. I had dusted off a Mary statue and, tip-toeing on a chair, was about to stand it on a shelf when Marge Blackman, the eighth-grade homeroom teacher, strolled in. She appeared to be in her mid-fifties and had short cropped brown hair, was neatly dressed, and seemed bright and perky.

"Mrs. Devilica said I was to be your mentor," she announced, smiling. "If you have any questions, just come to me." And that's just what I would do, dozens of times, in the coming months.

"I was a principal at St. Hilary's in Tappan County, which is where I live," she explained. "But I wanted to get back into the classroom and teach again, which is why I came here."

As I chatted with her I came to realize that there just might be something missing from her story. It made no sense to give up a job close to your home for one that was sixty miles of congested roads away and offered much less pay, but she seemed friendly enough and, anyway, what she chose to do with her life was her own business.

That evening, I was worried sick anticipating my first day with the students when I received a phone call from a friend that pushed the situation from bad to worse. Peter had been a teacher and principal in Catholic schools for years before becoming a public school teacher for twice the pay. He still had connections in the archdiocese and somehow seemed to have the scoop on everyone.

"Jimmy, I hate to tell you, but that principal you're working for is a bitch!" he began nervously. "Her whole school quit on her last year. She's a walking nightmare."

My stomach sank and the room seemed to become a roller coaster poised for a big descent.

"Now you tell me."

"I just found out. Try to stay on her good side if you want to stay there. God, I feel sorry for you," Peter said, sounding deeply sympathetic.

"Thanks."

"Don't worry, you're going to make a hundred mistakes, but you're new. They should allow for that," he said encouragingly, trying to put a positive spin on the terrible news. I realized the key word in his final sentence was "should."

After a night of fitful tossing and turning, I awoke at five with a sense of nervous anticipation. Even at this early hour the air was humid and oppressive and held the promise of a blazing hot noon. With great speed, I showered and dressed and arrived at the school at seven. The students would show up at eight. The final countdown began.

I raced around the room, putting the paper nameplates on the thirty desks, thinking that I would no more be able to remember them all then I could jump up and fly to the moon. And, to add to the horror, there were an additional fifty-two students in the sixth and eighth grades. Finally, at ten minutes to eight, I squared my shoulders and, with a hammering heart, marched down to the front lobby to join the other teachers awaiting the opening bell.

The office was packed with parents taking care of last minute arrangements and payments with the two very harried looking school secretaries. Nervously adjusting my tie to the point of almost choking, I joined the other eleven teachers crammed into the tiny entrance way, all of them animated and talking excitingly. Then Mrs. Devilica waddled out of the office armed with a large bell and we lined up like little kids behind her.

"Let's go," she commanded, leading the obedient line of teachers out the front door and into the parking lot to face a noisy sea of scattered blue and white uniforms. Then she lifted the heavy bell over her head and rang it loudly. Like magic, the students silently lined up in the parking lot by classes in what looked like a well-choreographed scenario. An interested audience of mothers observed from the far side of a chain-link fence. I walked over to the well-scrubbed and innocent looking seventh graders and smiled, unfortunately forgetting the admonition of not showing that gesture until Christmas.

Each class, beginning with pre-k, entered the school and paraded past the smiling principal and priest, who were positioned next to rosebushes in the entranceway. Why, this wasn't bad at all! I wondered if anything could be so warm and adorable. I led the parallel lines of kids, one of boys, the other of girls, up the stairs to my classroom and stood at the doorway. I said "good morning" to the students as they breezed by me into the classroom, the response of most being an averted head and a stony silence. Not exactly a great start, but I had seen many movies where the students were wary of the teacher at first but warmed up quickly, so I was sure the situation would turn around shortly.

Inside the room, the students had seated themselves at their designated desks and were talking non-stop. I began to take attendance and mispronounced many of the last names. The students were laughing so hard I wondered if I would have been better off being a stand-up comic. I wished all their surnames were Smith of Jones. Then I tried to talk about what we would be doing in class that year, yet no one was paying an iota of attention to me.

"Hey, quiet down!" I finally screamed, exasperated. No effect. I walked over to the wall and shut off the lights. No one even noticed. I was running out of all the tricks my teaching friends had told me to use to calm the class and get their attention.

I remembered the nun in my childhood catechism class used to tell us that at twenty minutes before every hour and twenty minutes after, every group naturally quiets down because that's when the guardian angels come down from heaven. I looked at the clock with longing. It was a quarter to the hour. I would never make it to the next angel visitation.

"I'm sending a note home to all your parents!" I shouted with a snarl. Sensing that I meant it, the students finally shut up for a short time.

By now the room had become a blast furnace. I was streaming perspiration and my shirt was soaked and stuck to my body. To add to the discomfort, I hadn't thought to bring in a bottle of water and my throat was parched. The students began asking to go to the bathroom or to get a drink of water. I gladly let them and wished that they stayed there!

The morning seemed interminable. I handed out the textbooks and fliers from the office, all amid a rising tide of talking. I wondered how the formerly sweet faces in front of me, the group of quiet, polite kids that I had met during my presentation last spring, could have suffered such a sea change over the summer and emerged as miniature monsters. I was just seconds from running screaming out the door and down the street to my car to speed away to the sanctuary of home when Mrs. Devilica suddenly appeared at the door and fixed the students with a deadly stare. Though the scene resembled more a visit from the hounds of hell than from heaven's angels, it silenced the students instantly. I found out then that, in a school setting, fear meant power.

Mrs. Devilica nodded at me and left, and I took quick advantage of the lull to pass out maps of the USA with the states outlined but not labeled. Having read that students know little about geography, I intended to see just how many states they could identify. Strolling around the room observing their answers, I was shocked. Most couldn't even find New York. One labeled it Florida. Wishful thinking in the winter.

By the time the sweltering morning ended, I was soaked to the skin and my patience had been pushed to the breaking point. I lined the students up and led them down the steps and out the front door into the blazing sunshine. Their parents were waiting for them at the fence. They were welcome to have them. I wanted to make a beeline for the nearest bar. Instead, I went back to the classroom and, exhausted, erased the blackboard.

On the second day of school the situation improved infinitesimally. The students switched classes and I got to meet the sixth and eighth graders. The sixth graders were still little kids and, for the most part, sweet and enthusiastic. The eighth graders were a different story entirely. Some seemed nice and, as the year went by, teaching them was an unmitigated treat. Others can only be described as a collection of rude zombies that had, at the tender age of fourteen, developed a cold hatred of the world for no discernable reason. Between these two extremes there seemed no be no middle ground, and the impressions I formed of these students the first day I met them was the same on the day of their eagerly awaited graduation.

I realized right away that if I wanted to keep the attention of the class for more than a few seconds I had to be an entertainer. This must have been a "modern" teaching strategy, I surmised, as I couldn't recall any of my teachers going an inch out of their way to make a course more interesting. They expected you to sit there, shut up, and learn - or else! Any entertainer knows you need feedback from a responsive audience to put on a good show. From most of the eighth graders and a scattering of the sixth and seventh graders, what I received at first for my best efforts were dead fish stares. Trying to play off that was discouraging at best.

Attempting to churn up enthusiasm was child's play compared to controlling the classes. Dispensing discipline had not posed a problem for the teachers when I was in school. Each had a different tried and true method of keeping the class quiet and attentive. One threw blackboard erasers at our heads. Having decades of practice, her aim was unerring, and even the kids in the far reaches of the room got it right in the middle of their foreheads. Another had the "board of education," a menacing wooden weapon the shop teacher had magnanimously made for him. Any infringement of decorum on the part of a student was punished with a public paddling. The procedure consisted of the teacher pulling out the chair from behind his desk and placing it in the front of the room. The kid being punished for bad behavior bent over the chair and got whacked. If the victim happened to be female, the happy-faced teacher would rub his hands together in glee while glancing at the boys in a bizarre attempt at male bonding.

My high school math teacher, who just happened to be an ex-Marine sergeant, administered the most sadistic form of discipline. If you were a boy, he would turn his college ring around and smack you hard with the blue stone in the back of the head. Girls got to squat down and do the duck walk up and down the aisles between the desks until their dignity and self-esteem was in shreds. If he was in a really mean mood and noticed our minds were not on math, all the windows in the room were flung open on frigid winter days so that we would freeze while he, clad in a warm wool coat, chuckled.

But for total, scarred-for-life level emotional pain, nothing could top what a nasty nun did to my friend Tommy while he was in the sixth grade at Our Lady of Lourdes. Tommy desperately had to pee but was too terrified to ask scary Sister Brigid for permission to go to the boys' room. A spreading yellow puddle of shame soon appeared under his desk, the tell-tale sign that he had peed his pants. That embarrassment alone would have haunted him forever, but an enraged Sister Brigid completed his humiliation by making Tommy go to the boys' room and rinse out his underwear. Then, for the coup de grâce, she had him leave his once white but now stained badge of shame on the radiator in the classroom, in full view of his amused classmates, for the remainder of the agonizingly endless afternoon. Poor Tommy's savior in this situation was his understanding mother, and a few days later he was sitting at a desk next to me at Clearwater Elementary.

As despicable as these methods were, they did get the desired results. I knew if I tried them now, though, I would be fired fast and arrested soon after.

Deprived of the use of flying erasers, swinging boards, concussion-causing class rings, and spirit-breaking humiliation, I was left with weapons that generally blunted in my hands, such as screaming, threats of detention, and sending students to the office. In the Bible, Luke says to "suffer the little children," but he couldn't have meant that admonition to apply to a class of seventh graders, so I consulted Mrs. Devilica on the office method.

"Send a student down to me to use as an example. See if that works," she suggested, probably basing this tactic on the Chinese proverb, "kill one, frighten 10,000." Staring at her scary face, I figured it was a sure bet. What student would want to sit across from that horror if there was any way to avoid it? The next day I decided to take her up on her invitation.

One seventh-grade student, Danny, just couldn't keep quiet or still. I would reprimand him and his motor mouth would shift into neutral for a moment, then go back into high gear. Marge, my mentor, heartily agreed with my choice.

"You mean the one with the glasses who looks like Harry Potter? He's driving me crazy," she spit out. "Send him down there soon. And he can take some of my eighth graders with him." That settled the matter, and our hapless Harry Potter look-alike was setup for sacrifice.

I felt it only fair to give warning to the class first, so, right after the morning prayer, I raised my finger and threatened, "The first person I see talking when I'm trying to teach is going to be sent down to Mrs. Devilica."

Then, softening, I continued, "Now I don't want to do this, so please don't make me. Take out your Social Studies books and open to page twenty."

As soon as I started explaining the reason for the delightful custom of human sacrifice by the Aztecs, Danny turned in his seat and began gabbing to the kid behind him. That was the proverbial last straw.

"Danny, take your books and go down to Mrs. Devilica's office," I ordered. The amazing thing is, he did.

That scene quieted the class for the rest of the session. We proceeded in the text to where

Montezuma gets slaughtered when Carol, one of the women working in the office, appeared at the door and called me over.

"Mrs. Devilica wants you to go down and get Danny. I'll watch your class while you're gone."

Thanking her, I left the room listening to laughter, sure that I heard one of the students saying, "She probably ate Danny".

I descended quickly to the lobby and spotted a very downcast Danny slumped on the bench. Mrs. Devilica, dressed that day in green and standing over him with a fiery face, looked like an imitation of Godzilla ready to incinerate him.

"Now tell Mr. Consorte that you're sorry," she screamed. A teary-eyed Danny looked up at me and heeded her command.

"I'm sorry, Mr. Consorte," he said in a prepubescent, strangled voice. A hard lump instantly formed in my throat and I felt like the biggest ogre of all time.

"You can go back to the classroom, and I don't want to see you down here again!" Mrs. Devilica said, and, case closed, she turned and waddled away.

I led Danny back to my classroom, hot tears stinging my eyes, and, realizing neither of us could appear in front of the class in our present condition, stopped in the stairwell.

"Danny, do me a favor. Don't make me do this to you again. Don't talk when I'm talking, okay?"

He nodded, and I realized then that I would get absolutely no pleasure out of being the person in power.

One practice in the school was to give out demerits for bad behavior. They were small slips of paper with three lines for the student's name, the date, and the reason for the demerit. They had to be taken home and, hopefully, signed by a parent, not forged by a student, before being brought back the next day. Three of them got you a dreaded detention. The receiving of one was never met with the clapping of hands and delight. To soften the blow, I tried to put them in a historical content.

"West Point has a demerit system. It's almost impossible to go through four years without getting at least one. In fact, only one cadet was ever able to do this. He later became very famous. Can anyone guess who he was?"

One boy raised his hand and answered, "Adolf Hitler."

"No. Hitler wasn't even an American, to say the least. It was Robert E. Lee, who later became a famous general during our Civil War." I really had my work cut out for me.

The first time I gave out a demerit was dreadful. The student, Sandy, was a sweet kid, but, when it came to talking, self-control was not even a consideration. I warned her one last time then wrote out a demerit and handed it over.

"Have it signed and bring it back to me tomorrow," I told her. She looked up at me with pleading, tear-filled eyes. I tried to pretend that I didn't care and continued teaching about Saint Anne and how you can still see her head at Lyons, France, conveniently skipping the fact that there are competing heads in Bologna, Sicily, and Germany.

Sandy was still in tears as I led my homeroom students through the hallway toward the front door at dismissal. I was doing my best to ignore her, and the front door was only a few feet away when I caved. As we passed the nurse's office, I waved Sandy inside.

"Are you sorry for talking?" I asked. She nodded her head in affirmation.

"Then give me that demerit," I said, and, with an audible sigh of relief, she took it out of her pocket and handed it to me.

"Oh, thank you, thank you," she gushed, her eyes gleaming with gratitude. Although I knew what I did was probably wrong if my goal was discipline, being only human it felt good to be someone's hero of the moment.

Sandy's gratitude wasn't feigned as the next morning I found an envelope on my desk with a thank you note inside. It said how I was the nicest teacher ever, and I prayed that she would follow through with her promise to keep quiet as it would now be almost impossible to present her with another demerit.

But once I gave out the first demerit the ice was broken. Dishing out others came easy, with any guilt on my part being dulled by repetition. A show of dubious enjoyment was even made of the punishment, as the demerit was presented to the miscreants while Connie Francis belted out the final verses of "Who's Sorry Now" on my CD player.

> *Right to the end*
> *Just like a friend*
> *I tried to warn you somehow*
> *You had your way*
> *Now you must pay*
> *I'm glad that you're sorry now*

The true litmus test of my disciplining skills came the next week when I had to take my class to the church for First Friday Mass. The teacher was supposed to lead the class at the front of the line, but I learned early on that as soon as my back was turned all hell would break loose behind me. If I turned around to reprimand the students while walking, I ran the risk of tripping and falling in front of them. To avoid this total humiliation, I positioned myself at the back of the line, which afforded me a clear view, and I could pounce on any person misbehaving. After giving the students a headful of admonitions as to their conduct in church, the line lurched down the hallway.

After seating them with a boy-girl-boy-girl arrangement in hopes of stemming most of the talking, I sat behind them in a pew with regular church attendants who, judging by their age, could have been guests at the Last Supper. Surprisingly, everything went well right through the communion. Then, when we all rose and began singing "Let There Be Peace on Earth," one of the old ladies in my pew, who must have skimped on her Poligrip that morning, lost an artificial piece of her anatomy. Her false teeth flew out of her mouth and onto the pew in front of her, directly between two of my standing students.

Their screams of shock startled the rest of the class, who quickly turned to see what was happening. The scene that met their eyes was that of an old woman desperately trying to retrieve her teeth while the students in the pew scrambled to get away from them. Then, with the suddenness of a detonated bomb, the kids exploded with laughter, and my valiant attempt to quiet them was in vain. Finally, the humiliated grandma got her teeth back in her mouth and fled out the front door, but the damage had been done. I could see Mrs. Devilica in a nearby pew, her eyes as big as saucers, and knew that she would pounce on my class and me in a moment.

I lined the class up quickly and we made a dash for the front door, figuring we could outdistance her lumbering stride. We got outside and rapidly headed toward the school. Looking back, I saw no sign of her and, thinking we were safe, breathed a quick sigh of relief. Then, as we were moving swiftly past the side door of the church, it suddenly swung open, revealing a vicious looking Mrs. Devilica. We had been cut off at the pass.

"How dare you!" she screamed at the students. Then she started in on me without offering me a chance to explain the situation. "Mr. Consorte, can't you control your class?"

I was so embarrassed at being yelled at in front of the students that I just stood there as if turned to stone. Shock strangled any reply, thank God, because she would have been the recipient of a string of curses. I wasn't twelve years old like my students and I seriously resented being treated like I was.

"Take them back to the classroom," she commanded, "and have them each write a paper titled 'Why I Should Not Talk in Church.' I want those papers in my office before lunchtime!" Then, to our collective relief, she turned and stamped back into the church.

When the papers were handed in, I checked them for content before sending them to the office. The students' reasons for not talking in church again ranged from the religious ("It is disrespectful to God") to the practical ("I don't want to get in trouble"). I had Danny bring them to Mrs. Devilica and prayed that the next time we went to church we would be seated far away from people who were in peril of falling apart.

What made the disciplining particularly difficult was that the students weren't allowed to talk anywhere on the school grounds: not in the classroom, the hallways, or even in the schoolyard after the bell rang. I tried reasoning with the kids at first. After all, in the former adult business and social circles that I had inhabited, if you were nice and respectful with people they generally treated you in a like manner. I was realizing quickly that the rules had changed. For one thing, you couldn't reason with thirteen-year-old kids. Any seasoned parent could have clued me in on that. Sad to say, it seemed that the nicer I was the worse they behaved. My kindness was taken as a sign of weakness to be eagerly exploited. I consulted Marge on the subject one morning in her classroom before school started and explained my dilemma.

"When the kids start crying, I feel terrible," I told her.

"When I make a student cry, I feel triumph!" she crowed. "Some of these kids are obnoxious, especially the eighth graders, so don't let them walk all over you, because they will if they can." Then she pointed out another potential problem by gesturing toward some parents gathered at the parking lot fence talking to each other while waiting for school to start.

"That spells trouble," she said with the conviction of one who has spent years dealing with difficult mommies and daddies. Subsequent events were to prove her prediction all to true.

Some of the parents were only too happy, or too stupid, to undermine whatever discipline we did dish out. One big brute of a girl, Mattie, was determined to do whatever she wanted, whenever she wanted. During the next few days, both Marge and I were forced to deal with her furious beast of a mother.

My turn came first. I warned Mattie many times to stop talking. Finally, I gave her a demerit, for which I received a dirty stare for the rest of the day. I was called down to the office that afternoon.

"Mattie's mother called and complained that you gave Mattie a demerit when she wasn't talking," said Mrs. Devilica.

"Why would I give anyone a demerit unless they deserved it?" I asked rhetorically, aware that she knew I hated to give them out even when the students more than deserved them.

"Well, that's what Mattie's mother said, so I told her I would let the demerit go this time."

"Fine", I thought, aware once again that she had undermined my authority. I didn't know what to make of her, as her decisions constantly contradicted themselves. But, not willing to risk a confrontation that could only cause me more problems, I let the whole thing slide and suffered in silence the smug look of triumph on Mattie's face for the rest of the day. Now, after experiencing an enabling parent, I fully realized why some kids behaved the way they did.

I moved Mattie's seat to my version of Siberia - a corner in the back of the classroom- surrounded her with students with whom I sensed she had nothing in common, and paid her perfunctory attention for the rest of the year.

This was minor-league stuff compared to what Mrs. Blackman went through the next day, although she brought it on herself and made me wonder what inner demons drove her to do what she did.

My class was lined up in the hallway, chattering away while waiting to switch classes with Marge's. I told them to stop talking or they were all getting demerits. With that threat, they calmed down, with the exception of Mattie. No surprise there as the day before had proved that she could do what she wanted with impunity. Suddenly, Marge struck, screaming, "Didn't you hear him tell you to stop talking?" She grabbed Mattie's wrist in a hard grip and dragged her into her classroom, leaving my class and I staring in silent shock. I knew you were never supposed to touch a student, so it was hard to believe what I had just witnessed. And of all students to pick to get physical with, her choice couldn't have been worse.

I led her class into my room and, to distract them from the show in the hallway, started teaching quickly, although the attack on Mattie was a tough act to follow. Fortunately, we were in the middle of the chapter on the Old West, so, thinking that violence and trashy behavior would distract them from what they had just witnessed, we discussed cowboys, gamblers, gunfighters, and saloon girls. When our classes switched back at the end of the period, I pretended nothing had happened and didn't even glance at Mattie. My class packed up, said a quick Hail Mary, marched out, and the day was over. Five minutes later, Mrs. Devilica's voice was on the PA system.

"Mrs. Blackman, please report to the office." Bad news sure travels with the speed of light in a school.

A short time later, while I was at my desk correcting homework, trying to decipher some student's handwriting that resembled hieroglyphics, a breathless and visibly upset Marge burst into the room.

"What's wrong?" I asked innocently, having a good idea exactly what was wrong and wanting to know the gory details.

"Mrs. Silas was in the office with Mrs. Devilica and she was livid," she said. "Mattie had told her that I twisted her arm and it left a bruise, but when Mrs. Devilica asked to see the bruise, Mattie said that it had gone away." She suddenly sat down at a student's desk as if the strength in her legs had given out.

"Are you all right?" I asked, concerned. She nodded her head a few times and I felt somewhat relieved that she wasn't about to drop dead in front of me.

"Mrs. Silas said that she wants to report me to the archdiocese," Marge continued. "I told her all I did was hold her sleeve and bring her into my classroom."

I just stared, almost amused, at her blatant lie.

"She's going to call some of your students down to the office tomorrow to get their stories on what happened. If she asked you what happened, what will you say?" she asked, instantly putting me on the spot. Marge, thus far, had been both kind and helpful to me, and I didn't want to see her in trouble or fired. Mattie was a sneaky pain-in-the-neck, and her mother seemed slightly deranged. But was Marge worth a mortal sin? After a quick mental struggle with morals I responded.

"I didn't really see anything, as I was trying to keep the kids quiet," I lied, taking the coward's way out and planning to beat a path to the confession booth as soon as possible.

Some of the seventh-grade girls were called down to the office the next day to give their deposition on the Mattie manhandling. In the end, Mattie's mother was somehow mollified, probably by being given a deep discount on tuition. That method, I was to learn, was generally used to end unsavory situations. I never did find out for sure, or care, because by now I was becoming a bit disillusioned by my discovery of strange personality quirks displayed by some of the adults at the school. I was to witness worse situations as the year wore on, and all of them would be carefully hidden and hushed up.

About a week after the Mattie incident, Carol, whose appearance at my door I now considered the portent of doom, was back again, walking in on an eighth-grade Social Studies test on the Old West. By now, I had decided to bring music into the curriculum so that the students would become familiar with songs from the different time periods. Carol entered the room to the sound of Patsy Montana singing "I Want to Be a Cowboy's Sweetheart." As before, she told me to go to the office while she watched my class. "Not another problem," I thought, sighing.

"I should have worn my cowboy hat," she smiled. "Mrs. Devilica wants to see you in the office right now. Maybe you should bring a six-shooter," she joked.

"Or a branding iron," I added with a rude reference to Mrs. Devilica's uncanny resemblance to a heifer. Carol had, on occasion, got in some digs about Mrs. Devilica, so I knew I was safe making such a comment. I left her laughing and took the trail to the office.

Mrs. Devilica was seated at her desk and Melanie, a nice little girl in the sixth grade, was nervously standing next to her.

"Go ahead, tell Mr. Consorte what you told me," Mrs. Devilica said to Melanie.

"Ivan Jovic told me to wipe his ass and suck his dick," came the incredible words out of a deceptively innocent mouth. She emphasized the words with dramatic, descriptive gestures, which were unnecessary, as I was more than aware of the meaning of both acts.

"And this happened in Mr. Consorte's classroom?" asked Mrs. Devilica, like a lawyer with a leading question.

"Yes," Melanie answered.

"Did you see this occur?" Mrs. Devilica demanded, fixing me with an accusing eye, as if the situation was somehow all my fault.

"No, or I certainly would have taken care of it," I replied, annoyed.

"Well, call his mother right now and tell her what happened," she commanded.

I searched through the record cards for Mrs. Jovic's telephone number, wondering what had happened to the world. When I was twelve, I had no idea what a sex act was. My mother had told me that it took a "father's love" to make a baby, and that sounded fine, whatever it meant. At thirteen, I learned the truth. During a baseball game, while my friend Chuck and I were waiting our turn up at bat, he whispered to me how babies really came to be. I just looked at him, speechless with horror, while he giggled, loving my reaction to his gross revelation.

"My parents would never do that!" I finally blurted out, thinking it was the ickiest thing I had ever heard.

I flatly refused to believe Chuck and accused him of lying, but an embarrassing discussion with my father that evening proved him correct.

Even if a boy did know a "dirty word" back then, you certainly didn't say it to a girl. One boy in my sixth-grade class had the stupidity to do just that and paid with a punishment of pain and humiliation, delivered with gusto by the gym teacher. As he was the only male teacher in the school, Mr. Fusco was honored with the task.

After having the sixth-grade boys in the gym class form a circle, he made the scared student, Jeffrey, stand in the middle of it with him.

"How dare you say those words to a girl! In Italy, they'd hang you for that," he screamed, looking at Jeffrey with utter contempt. "Bend over," he ordered, and when Jeffrey complied, a size twelve sneaker attached to Mr. Fusco's foot found its mark, sending Jeffrey flying out of the circle. That settled the matter. Jeffrey didn't cry. Boys weren't supposed to cry in the 1950s. He also didn't curse in front of a girl in school again. None of the boys did, as no one wanted to be next in that circle.

But that was all in a time long past. Now we notified parents. I found Ivan's home number and called, wondering how to tactfully tell a mother that her boy just told a little girl to suck his dick.

Ivan's grandmother, speaking in a thick accent that bespoke the mist-shrouded mountains of some Eastern European country, answered the phone. "Ivan's mother at work. You call work number. Ivan all right?"

"Yes, everything is fine," I said with a cheer I was far from feeling. "I just have some information to give her."

I called Mrs. Jovic's office number and hoped that she wasn't having a bad day at work. If so, it was about to get much worse.

"Oh, good afternoon, Mr. Consorte," she said sweetly. "Is everything all right?"

"Well, not exactly, and I hate to have to tell you this," I said sincerely. Then I blurted out quickly what Ivan said, glad to get it over with.

"Oh, dear. I'm so sorry," she said sadly. "I know that Ivan is new there this year and is having some problems fitting in. Sometimes he goes about things the wrong way."

"Yes, well, this is totally unacceptable behavior. The girl is very upset," I explained.

"I promise I will talk to Ivan, and I can certainly assure you something like this will never happen again," Mrs. Jovic said reassuringly, and I believed her.

"I'll also try to do what I can to, uh, help him," I responded, which, translated, meant moving his seat as far away as possible from Melanie and praying that, in the future, Ivan kept a lid on his potty mouth.

It didn't help. Ivan bothered everyone he sat next to, and I was constantly moving him to different desks. To make matters worse, he had the annoying habit of picking his nose and laughing to himself. This strange show was too good to miss, and he acquired a large and interested audience as the kids would focus their attention on his antics, their faces alternating between expressions of amusement and revulsion. Finally, feeling paranoid, Ivan would yell, "What are you looking at?" That got the age-appropriate response of, "Nothing much."

Poor Ivan had serious problems, and I felt sorry for him and his family. But his silliness was certainly making my classroom control situation much more difficult, and my anguished prayers to St. Dymphna for a miraculous improvement in Ivan were ignored. The only break I got from Ivan that year was when his parents took him to their faraway homeland for the funeral of a close relative, whose long final rest afforded me a brief but happy one.

Trying to keep my head straight amid all this insanity was hard enough, but I soon realized that, as a sea of students swarming with germs surrounded me, my physical health was also at serious risk. A big mistake was having placed a box of Kleenex on top of my desk for the kids to use at their discretion. This was an open invitation for anyone desiring an audience to blow their nose loudly in front of their classmates, as well as in my face. They got the desired screams of "Oh, gross!" for their theatrics while I came down with a deadly cold that seemed to last forever. The box of Kleenex was soon relegated to a corner in the back of the room next to a Jesus statue. If facing their savior didn't deter them from their dramatics, at least putting the length of the room between their nose-propelled germs and my face certainly couldn't hurt my health. But, because washing their hands was too much work for the kids, and I was constantly handling things they had touched, "cooties" and the accompanying illnesses would be a continuous job hazard.

And it wasn't my own illnesses I had to deal with. One morning, while I was in the middle of telling the American History class that Iroquois shamans would stick a piece of wood down their throats and puke on their patients, thereby "curing" them of their illness, Carol appeared at my door with another dilemma.

"Robert is in the boys' room very sick. Mrs. Devilica is afraid that if he passes out he'll hit his head on the floor. She wants you to go in there and watch him until his mother comes to pick him up. She's on her way now," she said. Then, lowering her voice so that her words only reached my ears, she hissed, "I'm glad to get out of that office for a while. That bitch has been riding me all morning."

"I hear you," I replied sympathetically, knowing she was referring to Mrs. Devilica. I tried to envision what it would be like to be stuck all day in the small confines of the office with that grouch, and the picture that appeared in my mind was far from pretty.

"Am I going to be scalped in here?" Carol asked, spotting the teepee set up in the front of the classroom, complete with a seventh grader squatting in front in an Indian costume and feathered headdress.

"No, we only burn people at the stake," I joked. "Class, start your homework until I get back. Chief Chicken Wing, go back to your desk for now," I told Tommy, the honorary Indian of the day. Then I hit the switch on the CD player and the song "Running Bear Loves Little White Dove" began to play.

"Running bare?" laughed Carol, the corners of her eyes crinkling.

"Running Bear! This is a Catholic school." I smiled and sped down the hall, hoping Robert hadn't slipped into a coma during the delay.

When I entered the boys' room, I saw a stall occupied. "Robert, are you O.K?" I asked. Between vomiting noises a voice croaked out something that sounded like "yes."

"Your mother is on her way to get you. If you need anything, I'll be right here in the meantime," I replied reassuringly, hoping that nothing more would be required than having to endure the repugnant odor. So, we waited for his mother. And waited. And waited some more.

"Where's your mother coming from, China?" I finally asked.

"She's only fifteen minutes away. She should be here soon," Robert replied before retching again. Trying to pass the time, I went to the mirror and primped, combing my hair and adjusting my tie. Finally, after what seemed an eternity, Robert's concerned mother, an attractive young woman, entered the bathroom.

"I'm sorry I took so long," she said, smiling sweetly. "I got caught in traffic."

"It's nice to meet you, Mrs. Bliss," I said politely. We chatted for a moment as if we were at a cocktail party and not standing in a smelly bathroom with a seriously sick kid. Then we remembered Robert and the reason we were there in the first place.

"Robert, can you come out and your mother will take you home?" I asked.

"I think so," was his weak reply. Mrs. Bliss and I continued our conversation while Robert dressed himself, flushed the toilet, and emerged from the stall, looking like the wrath of God.

"I hope you feel better," I said as his mother walked him down the stairs, and I wondered why dealing with strange situations and sick students didn't appear in the job description.

Because I arrived at school over an hour before it opened, I would sometimes use the same second floor boys' room. The downstairs one for the younger kids had tiny urinals and sinks that were hard to use, and the one for the teachers to use was locked at that time. One morning, on the way out of the bathroom, I saw "Fuck Mrs. Devilica" written in large black letters on the door. "Who would want to?" was my first irrelevant thought, grateful that it didn't say "Fuck Mr.

Consorte." Then I matured a bit and realized it had
to be removed before the students arrived. The only
other person in the school at that hour was Jose, the
janitor, and he was the person I needed to see anyway
as he had the materials to remove the offensive
remark. I went searching the school for Jose, annoyed
that this had to happen that morning when I had tests
to correct before school started.

Finally spotting him in the gym, I was now stuck
with a serious language barrier. I spoke no Spanish
and he spoke no English. Fortunately, the act I had to
describe was common in all cultures, so I thought I
would be able to find some similar symbols.

"*Buenas noches*," I began, having somewhere
heard that statement and knowing it was some kind of
a greeting.

"In the boys' room, uh, *el mano lavatorie*,
someone wrote "Fuck Mrs. Devilica" on the *doro*."

"*Si?*" he replied, looking puzzled and shaking his
head.

"You know, fuck, fuck," I said, becoming
somewhat exasperated. Then I added some gestures
by giving the finger and performing pelvic thrusts.

"Mrs. Devilica," I continued, pointing to a door.
He got it.

"Oh, *follar* Mrs. Devilica," he smiled, showing
complete comprehension.

"Yes, yes," I said, relieved. "Let's go. I'll show you. He put down his broom and followed me to the bathroom. When we got there, I pointed to the door.

"See," I said.

"*Si*, fuck," he replied, nodding his head and saying something that sounded like he would take care of it.

"*Gracias, gracias*," I said, relief flooding me, and I raced back to my classroom just in time to hear the morning bell being rung.

When I went back into the boys' room after school that day, I saw that the words had been painted over. Two months later when this happened again, I just smirked and said nothing. By then I was in complete agreement with the author.

Soon after this incident, the same boys' room was the recipient of a very strange request. A former student, who went on to wealth and success in adulthood, paid the school a visit. While there, he specifically requested to see the second floor boys' room, and I was given the honor of granting his wish.

"This is fantastic, it looks exactly the same as when I was a student here," he gushed ecstatically. "I have such happy memories of this bathroom."

Who has happy memories of a school bathroom? I was tactful enough not to ask what went on in this bland, green-tiled lavatory to provide him with such loving nostalgic gratification, and I escorted him back to the office, where he presented Mrs. Devilica with a strange request. If she would always keep his treasured bathroom looking exactly the way it was, he would continuously pay for any repairs to it. The deal was struck and, to this day, when I see "Mr. Money" on TV doing commercials for his company, I wonder what happy events occurred decades ago in that bathroom that made it a candidate in his mind for historic preservation.

Besides dealing with behavior problems and diseases, I was also made aware early on that many of the students were "coming of age." One afternoon, when a group of girls were getting their backpacks from the closet in preparation for departing, I spotted some of them rolling up their skirts under their sweaters to shorten them. All I could think was "for these jerky boys?" as the seventh grade is an awkward age at best. I actually toyed with the idea of adding to our prayer selection the plead to Saint Ann, the patron of matrimony, that I remembered my giggling teenage girl cousins saying years ago: "Please, Saint Ann, send me a man." Then I quickly thought the better of it as it could be taken in a totally different context than marriage. I cringed as I imagined the lurid headline in the newspaper: "Catholic School teacher makes students pray for sex," and I would soon be praying from a prison cell to St. Dismas for an early probation. So we stuck with the much safer "hope of heaven" harmless type prayers, and the girls were left to their own devices of allure-skirts rolled up an inch, notes passed in class, and the like.

It was only October, but I was beginning to sense that something was very wrong with my relationship with both Mrs. Blackman and Marlene. Marge's moods would change swiftly. One moment she would be smiling and accommodating to me, then the next moment, with seemingly no provocation, she would lash out in fury.

I usually played music on a CD player in my classroom in the morning while I prepared for the day before the arrival of the students. The selections ranged from classical to songs from the 1950s, certainly nothing loud or obnoxious. The music served the dual purpose of soothing me before the crazy day began and drowning out the high-pitched voices coming from Mrs. Blackman's classroom across the hall as she and Marlene loudly bitched about the students, parents, and principal while they chowed down McDonald's breakfast specials.

One morning as I sat at my desk correcting papers, desperately trying to find some credit to give to a student's awful essay, Marge, with a McDonald's bag in one hand and a tote bag decorated with a pencil and apple in the other, passed by my room. Suddenly, she stopped, glared at me, and screamed, "Why do you have to play music?" Fortunately, she then raced to her room before I could respond, because I would have told her to go somewhere, the destination being far from heaven. It was obvious now that whatever demons drove her to lash out didn't discriminate between students and adults. She apologized to me later that day, but the damage had been done.

As for Marlene, I received only icy stares and one-word responses to my attempts at camaraderie. Whatever personality she had was encased in a hard shell that seemed impossible to crack. I remembered her "true confessions" at our first meeting about her miserable childhood and the kids making fun of her because she was overweight. Her current dissatisfaction with her appearance and situation in life made her a teacher version of Dickens' Miss Havisham, a woman seeking revenge on her students to compensate for past wrongs committed against her by others. She could often be extremely nasty, so I thought it best to show her perfunctory courtesy and keep a safe distance.

One warm October afternoon after dismissal, while I was resetting the plastic figures in my Ben-Hur Coliseum Playset that was displayed in front of the blackboard, Carol strolled into my classroom.

"Can I play?" she questioned, smiling.

"Look at this?" I said, pointing to

the figures of the lions attacking helpless people and gladiators lying on top of slave girls. "The students always rearrange these figures when I'm not looking."

"Now you can see what's on their minds - gore and sex," she laughed, picking up a three-inch tall gladiator and running a finger slowly over his big biceps.

"I'd rather have their little minds on their studies," I responded.

"Yeah, well good luck," Carol wished me, putting down the figure, whatever fantasy she briefly savored finished.

"Anyway, I just wanted to thank you. Michael is having the time of his life working on that pretty house and painting the figures of the people in skirts," she said, referring to a project I had given to her son, a student in my sixth-grade class.

"It's the Greek gods and temple diorama," I said, trying to smother a grin.

"Well, whatever it is. How the hell would I know? History was my worst subject," she confessed.

"I'm glad he's enjoying it. He's a good student and a wonderful kid. Sometimes I'll lose my place in the Social Studies book and I'll ask him, 'Michael, what page are we on?' He always knows just where we left off. If everyone in his class were like him, my job would be a dream," I said, smiling, and I meant every word.

"There's something I have to tell you," she said, suddenly serious. "You're a nice, polite guy and you're good to my son, and I don't think what's going on is right."

"What's going on?" I asked apprehensively.

"Well, just be careful what you say to Marge and Marlene," she warned while looking me straight in the eye. "They keep pumping the kids for information about what goes on in your class. Some of them told their mothers about it and they complained about them to Mrs. Devilica."

"But what do they have against me, I never did anything to them?" I asked, confused and upset.

"I know, I know. But between you and I, and don't ever repeat this," she pleaded.

"Scout's honor," I said, raising my hand in a burlesque of the old Boy Scout sign.

"I think they're jealous of you," Carol said, dropping her voice. "Both of them are, because the students enjoy your classes and not theirs."

"Then they should make their classes more entertaining and shut up," I shot back, hurt and angry.

"I know, I know," Carol agreed, attempting to sooth me. But her next words only caused more misery.

"Plus, they badmouth you down in the office, and I don't like to hear stuff like that, you know what I mean? It's not right. Just be careful what you say to them."

Her warning left me more disappointed than indignant, a disappointment hard to analyze, the disappointment of a child seeing illusions crumble.

"I've worked in many offices where all the people ever did was gossip and cause trouble, and for no good purpose. I thought that working in a religious school would be different, and this school seemed the nicest of all the schools where I had interviews," I said tiredly.

"Well, don't let the religion stuff fool you. This place can get pretty nasty. Last year, Mrs. Devilica drove the entire teaching staff out of here," Carol said, and if she had quoted Jeremiah's "Be horribly afraid" her words could not have been more prophetic.

"I'm beginning to realize that."

"Oh, and by the way, Marlene just got in trouble herself, so she's one to talk."

"What did she do?" I asked eagerly, hoping for the worst. The hell with that turning the other cheek stuff.

"She was in the room alone with Anthony in the sixth grade and had her arm around his shoulders. Allison in the sixth grade just happens to like him. She saw them together, got jealous, and told Mrs. Devilica," Carol crowed triumphantly.

"Good!"

"So, she shouldn't talk about others, because she's not so perfect herself," she said, picking up the plastic gladiator for another curious viewing.

"That's for sure," I agreed.

Carol glanced up at the wall clock. "I better get back to the office," she said with a slight sense of panic.

"And remember, just be careful," she warned again, absently putting the gladiator back in the arena and racing out of the room. I returned to fixing the figures in the coliseum when I noticed Carol had placed her gladiator stabbing another in the back. Suddenly I wondered if it was a coincidence or her subconscious at work.

By now, I was beginning to wonder why I was teaching. So far, the experience had turned out to be nothing like the idyllic scenario I had anticipated. Instead of kind and supportive co-workers and eager students hanging on my every word, I endured fellow teachers and a principal who were tortured by inner demons and kids with all kinds of incomprehensible problems. And the weekends were no cause for celebration either, as Saturdays were spent running errands that couldn't be done during the workweek, and Sundays were filled with the fun of correcting papers and doing a plan book. Any semblance of a social life was shattered until Christmas vacation.

Nor could I come home each evening to blessed surcease, as a woman with a two hundred-pound, schizophrenic adult son purchased the co-op unit above me and the son remained awake all night, pacing the floor directly over my head. Earplugs, a humming fan, and sleeping pills provided little relief. The only time I got a break was when he would direct a scary, screaming tirade against his mother and would be hauled off to a mental home for a month. But he always returned to haunt me once again. I got no rest on my pillow unless I slept in my car or plagued friends to put me up for the night at their place. Neither was a long-term solution to the problem, but both methods did manage to stave off a complete exhaustive collapse.

Despite all this, I actually enjoyed the teaching part of the job and tried to make my classes entertaining and meaningful. Remembering all too well the four bare walls and boring textbooks with few pictures in the classrooms of my youth, I turned my room into a historic version of the Macy's windows at Christmas. It was decorated for every time period that we were studying in history. Plastic soldier sets from all periods of history were set up and played with during indoor recess by the students, G.I. Joe dolls, both male and female, stood stiffly at attention on my desk, and video clips of movies and material recorded from the History Channel were used to visually reinforce what I was teaching verbally. The sometimes serious, sometimes silly, visual show had started.

Chapter 5

**If You Want to See Old Satan on the Run,
Come Along and See Just How it's Done**

I n an attempt to do for religion what I had done
for history, I made an online purchase of talking
Jesus and Mary dolls. Arriving home one evening,
I saw the box containing the holy toys and, excited, I
pulled open the cardboard to examine my purchase.

Each doll was dressed in their regulation religious
robes with serene expressions on their faces and their
arms spread wide. Both were boxed in maps of the
Holy Land, complete with Bethlehem, Jerusalem, and
assorted sacred bodies of water like the Jordan River
and Sea of Galilee.

I opened the Jesus doll first, pushed the button
in his back, and listened to a peaceful, measured
rendition of the Beatitudes. Wondering what Mary
had to say, I pushed her button and, instead of the
sweet voice I expected, she let out a piercing scream.

Trying to make some sense of the situation, I stupidly thought that maybe it was the doll's rendition of Mary's labor pains, or maybe her reaction to the slaughter of the innocents. I quickly pressed the button again and again, refusing to believe that I could have received a defective Mary. But she wouldn't stop screaming. Overwhelmed by superstition, I suspected that the doll was possessed and its head would start spinning around at any moment. With this fiend from hell screaming in my ear, my brain swirled with confusion. I began to panic, fearful that someone in my co-op building would think that I was committing murder and call the cops. Then an idea took form in my mind and grew swiftly. With Mary in hand, I ran down the hallway to the deserted laundry room, flung the doll into a dryer, and slammed the door shut. The blood-curdling screaming was now barely audible, and the only problem I could foresee was that, if anyone came into the room and opened the dryer, there could be a very bizarre Mary sighting. Mobs of the misty-eyed devout and amused news crews would cram into the laundry room the next day to share in the miracle.

As soon as I arose the next morning, I went to the laundry room to see how Mary made out. There was no noise at all when I entered, and when I opened the dryer door she sat silently in her Holy Land box. I pushed her button again and again but got no response. I had received a defective Mary doll and was now determined to either get a refund or a replacement verbal Virgin.

I called the company that was located deep in the Bible belt and described the disturbing incident.

"Oh, dear me, why this has never happened before", sang a soft voice with a Southern accent. "We'll mail you another Mary tomorrow, and God bless."

She was as good as her word and a new Mary arrived two days later. With some trepidation I pressed the button in her back, but this time I was treated to a soft voice saying, "I am the Lord's servant." Satisfied that she was in good working order, I brought both dolls into school the next day and couldn't wait to demonstrate my new teaching tools to the students.

As the seventh-grade religion class was on the chapter about Jesus and Mary attending the wedding where the wine ran out, I decided to debut the dolls. With some ceremony, I took the holy dolls out of a bag, solemnly held them up in front of the class, and began pressing the buttons. Instead of the reverence I expected, the kids looked at me as if I had lost my mind. Then they began laughing hysterically. I realized that I had misjudged the age group the dolls were geared towards, so I quickly placed them on my desk between the nun doll and Pilgrim Barbie. Then

I calmed the class down and went back to the "water into wine" story.

The next day, I loaned the dolls to the first-grade class, where they were met with a more respectful reception. The teacher told me that, when the dolls talked, her small students stared in stunned silence at the modern, molded plastic miracle.

After the complete flop of my Jesus and Mary figures, I tried another tactic to enliven my religion classes. The sixth-grade religion curriculum contained all those warm and touching Old Testament stories, such as Cain bludgeoning his brother Abel to death, Abraham attempting to carve up his son, Jezebel being thrown out of a window and eaten by dogs, and David cutting off the head of Goliath, to name just a choice few. I decided that showing some religious films after teaching the facts from the textbook would serve the dual purpose of reinforcing the learning process and entertaining the students at the same time. It turned out to be a lot more entertaining than expected, or desired!

When we were on the chapter about Joseph (the one with the coat of many colors), one of my students brought in a video of the story, saying her mother said I could borrow it. I didn't have time to preview it but, remembering the harmless Bible movies of my childhood, I wasn't particularly concerned.

Just as the class finished reading the Joseph story, complete with his brutal brothers and his dreams of starving cows, Julissa raised her hand.

"Mr. Consorte," she cried in an aggrieved voice, "Steven picked his nose and put the booger on the back of my chair."

"No, I didn't," shot back Steven, suddenly looking as guilty as Cain. I walked over to the crime scene, spotted something dark and lumpy on the chair, and tried to figure out if it was indeed an offensive lump of Steven's snot. With no means to perform a chemical analysis, and with the memory of Steven's recent track record of transgressions, it was safe to assume he did the dirty deed. I cleaned the back of Julissa's chair with Windex and decided on punishment for the awful act. It was the perfect opportunity to try out my new method of psychological punishment, so I took the Barbie-sized nun doll that stood on my desk and put her on Steven's, her eyes staring accusingly at him.

"Leave her just like that for the rest of the class, and I hope she teaches you a lesson," I commanded.

"But she gives me the creeps," he cried.

"Good!" was my unsympathetic response as I walked over to the television and put in the *Joseph* DVD. As soon as my back was turned, I heard uproarious laughter in the room. Swirling around quickly, I caught a smirking Steven pulling up the nun doll's habit and peering beneath.

"He's looking for the good parts," yelled one of the boys in the back of the room.

"Nuns don't have good parts," laughed another.

"That's enough," I said in my best authoritative teacher voice, trying desperately to smother a smile as the nonsense reminded me of something my friends and I would have done at their age. "Leave your new girlfriend alone, Steven, and pay attention to the video."

The *Joseph* that I was showing had been a TV miniseries and featured Paul Mercurio playing a very muscular Joseph.

"Mr. Consorte, did Joseph go to a gym?" asked one of the boys who I knew was very much into sports.

"Well, I don't think he got his build herding sheep," I responded in an attempt to be amusing.

Things were going well until a scene where Leslie Ann Warren, playing Potiphar's wife, tries to seduce Joseph while he is bathing naked in a pool. I was getting really nervous, and for good reason. Where was the dream coat when you needed it? Suddenly, she reached down in the water and grabbed him, well, you know where. Joseph's response was a shocked look, but not as shocked as mine. My eyes were the size of saucers.

"What is she doing?" asked one of the girls, mystified.

"Oh, she's just looking for the soap," I lied, intensely relieved when the scene quickly ended and hoping none of the students would be asked that evening what they had learned in school that day.

A few weeks after the debacle of the *Joseph* movie, we were studying David. Stupidly, after having the close call with the last film, I rented a DVD starring Richard Gere. This time, I took the precaution of having the remote permanently planted in my hand. Anything objectionable could be zapped before anyone would really see it. The students enjoyed Goliath's decapitation, as I expected they would. Anything gory and morbid always grabbed their attention, and the movie was proceeding innocently enough when Marge came to the door to ask a question. Suddenly, we heard a boy cry out, "Oh my God, they're naked!" Marge prudently ran to her room, not wanting to be involved in a potential disaster, and I caught a glance of David's wedding chamber sequence before pressing the "next" button on the remote. My bad luck continued as the new scene began with a graphic rendition of a baby getting circumcised.

"What are they doing to the baby?" asked an acutely curious girl.

"Oh, there're just cutting off the baby's pinky toe. It's an old Jewish custom," I answered, thinking quickly.

"I don't think that was his toe they were cutting," said a boy with a slight build and a sly smile.

"Be quiet, Anthony," I shot back with a sharp glare.

I sweated this stupid mistake out and slept little that night. After all, I was supposed to be the arbiter of morals. But when no screaming parents swarmed into my room the next morning, I knew I was safe. I wonder to this day if the members of that class still think all Jewish boys are missing a pinky toe.

While giving a test on John the Baptist, I attempted to make it more relevant by showing Rita Hayworth as Salome doing the "Dance of the Seven Veils." The idea was ill-conceived, as I noticed that all the boys' eyes were riveted on the screen and concentration on the test was reduced to nothingness as other areas of their developing brains went into overdrive. As grades held a higher priority with me than entertainment, *Salome* was turned off before the third veil descended to the dance floor.

My last attempt at entertaining the class with a religious film was by showing *King of Kings* starring Jeffrey Hunter. Having seen this movie many times since childhood, I knew there were no offending sex scenes, so I was sure there would be no problems. We got to the crucifixion scene and the first nail was being hammered in when Shauna, a shouting Baptist, stood up from her seat, dramatically flung her forearm across her eyes, and screamed, "I can't watch it. I can't watch my savior being naaaaaaaaailed to the cross!"

"Then go the girls' room," I said, shocked at her dramatic outburst, and I decided then and there that the students and I would be spared any more religious films for the remainder of the year. Though the course would be a lot less entertaining, what was left of my nervous system would benefit immensely.

Chapter 6

Whoever Learns From Correction is Wise

A horrid suspicion dawned on me in my early days of teaching. Could it be possible that my students weren't all geniuses? The suspicion became fact after I mournfully viewed the mixed results of the first tests, which provided proof that their mental capabilities ranged from quite gifted to practically brain dead. I knew that I not only taught but also reviewed the material on the test, so what happened? You can't fail half a class. Of course, I blamed myself and came to the sorry conclusion that I was the worst teacher who ever stood before a blackboard.

I sought solace and, hopefully, a solution with my "mentor," Marge, even though I no longer trusted her and was guarded in any information I shared.

"The idiots did just as bad on my tests," she brutally blurted out as she scanned the names and grades on the group of tests I showed her. "They just don't want to put any effort into studying. Start keeping them in at lunchtime if they don't do their homework. And up the grades a few points where you can to get them a passing grade," she bluntly suggested. Then, as an afterthought, she added with a sharp look, "You didn't hear that from me."

The next time some of the students didn't do their homework, they stayed in at lunchtime doing an extra assignment and, as an added incentive not to repeat this punishment, listening to a CD of Tiny Tim's greatest hits. It was a toss-up as to who was tortured more, the homework delinquents or their teacher, but I was determined to improve their work and study habits, whatever the sacrifice may be. From that day forward, I would threaten another Tiny Tim performance then purse my lips, and the students would look at me in sudden anguished apprehension. All the homework was handed in on time for the next two months.

The solution to students getting better grades on their tests, aside from Marge's advice to just inflate the numbers, came from a source least expected. Danny, the talkative boy I had sent down to Mrs. Devilica as a deterrent to others, confided that he had a difficult time learning and asked if he could stay after school before the next test and get extra help. Duly impressed by his gumption, and finding Mrs. Devilica in a rare magnanimous mood, I was granted permission to tutor Danny that afternoon in the lobby of the school. We sat on the bench outside of the office when classes ended and went over the material, ad nauseam, until it finally sank in.

Danny's was the first paper I corrected after the test the next day, and his parents were delighted with the results. He improved an entire grade level. As it wasn't fair to give just Danny free tutoring, I offered it to his entire class on the day before each major test, and I soon had a roomful of students every time. And it was well worth the time and effort. The test scores rose, some noticeably, some infinitesimally, but at least all were headed in the right direction.

When the first quarter exams had been given and graded, I was thrilled that almost everyone had done well. It had taken an entire weekend working at my home computer to make the tests, and some had been done late at night when I was operating in what could best be described as an exhausted daze. Then they had been reviewed and passed on by Mrs. Devilica.

It was Halloween and we had the next day, All Saints Day, off. This provided a three-day weekend, and I was looking forward to catching up on things. The last period of the day was reserved for my homeroom's Halloween party. The mothers had made cupcakes and cookies, which were tantalizingly displayed on a table in the front of the room, waiting to be devoured. Then, just before the fun was to begin, the hideous blow fell.

Carol came into my classroom and wickedly whispered, "The big witch wants to see you in her office right away. Bring a stake and some matches."

"If I had them, I would," I replied, thinking that, if the past was any prediction, being called to the principal's loathsome lair couldn't possibly be good. Once in the office, I had hardly seated myself when the accusations started flying.

"I had a call from one of the parents that your seventh-grade religion test was rigged!" she screamed. "The answers in the workbook were in the same order as the questions."

When I recovered from the shock, I replied, "If that's how the answers came out, it certainly wasn't done on purpose. I'm surprised I didn't spot it." I wanted to add that I'm surprised she didn't spot the mistake also, as she had approved the tests. Instead, I sat there with my face reddening from suppressed fury.

"That invalidates all of the religion tests. They all have to be redone and given again on Monday. Now go tell the students that they all have to retake the tests," she commanded, her face contorted with rage, which didn't exactly flatter her less than lovely features.

That was it. I was too angry to argue and had to get out of there before I burst a blood vessel. I stood up, turned on my heel, and took off. When I reached the stairwell, my heart was hammering so hard from embarrassment and insult that I stopped to calm myself down and collect my thoughts. I knew that my news would not be met in the classrooms with cheering and a clapping of hands. When I looked God in the face on the Day of Judgment and read my sentence in His eyes, it would not be as bad as breaking this horrid news to the students. I took a moment to arrange my face into more placid lines, for I knew that I must look like a crazy man. Then I squared my shoulders, took a deep breath, and marched up the steps.

My unwelcome news was received with the predictable response.

"What?"

"You've got to be kidding!"

"How come?"

I had no good reason to give them and left the cause of their misery a mystery. I saved my homeroom for last, and the horrible news was mitigated by my giving a go to start the Halloween festivities.

None of the students seemed in the mood for a party at the moment, but once the goodies, gifts, and cards started going around, they bounced back. Kids live in the present and rarely give a passing thought to what the next day may bring. I received unexpected gifts and cards from the students, addressed to "my favorite teacher." Far from feeling like anyone's favorite teacher, I felt like a complete failure.

The entire weekend was wasted making up three new tests on my computer. The worse part was that I had used the best questions and essays on the last tests, which made composing these make-up tests tedious and extremely time consuming. They were finally finished on Sunday night at nine and I fell asleep as soon as my head hit the pillow.

Before the students arrived on Monday morning, I breezed into Mrs. Devilica's office with the new tests and was treated to her usual moody "Blue Monday" face.

"I've decided we're only going to re-give the essay questions. I'll have them typed separately and sent up to you," she said with a smirk, then turned her back to me.

Thank the Lord I lacked a weapon.

Chapter 7

There's No Place Like
School for the Holidays

With the fixed intention of departing for good at the end of that day, I sought out Marge during the lunch hour.

"I'm quitting," I blurted out, not caring if she did tell tales. By tomorrow it wouldn't matter because I would be just a memory.

"I'll clear everything out at the end of the day. I can't work for that witch. I'll miss most of the students, but I miss other people who were once part of my life and I've gotten by. Anyway, thanks for all the help and it was nice working with you," I said sincerely, except for the part about working with her.

"Well, I can't say that I blame you," she replied, somewhat sadly, probably contemplating the fact that my replacement might be far more disagreeable. "Actually, you're probably the lucky one, getting out.

They're all nuts here," she concluded, presenting to me a perfect example of the pot calling the kettle black.

With my mind made up to leave this loony bin for good in two hours, I picked up the students from the cafeteria. When the class filed into the room, two smiling boys came up to me. One was Danny, the student who had requested extra help, and the other was Johnny, a friend of his. Johnny daydreamed a lot and once had to be told to put away a computer game magazine he was reading in the middle of a class. Both were far from good students. I couldn't imagine what they wanted and, at this moment, I didn't really care.

"We really enjoy your history classes," began Danny, somewhat shyly.

"Yeah, I didn't like history before, but you make it fun," chimed in Johnny. "Do you think we could do some projects for extra credit, like maybe build a battle diorama on our lunch hour?"

I looked down at their earnest faces with wonder and was overcome with a lethal dose of Catholic guilt. My plan to go home for good was fast forgotten.

I told Mrs. Devilica the next morning of Danny and Johnny's request and, surprisingly, she said yes. Either I had caught her at the crest of a menopausal mood swing, the aftermath of a night of wild desires fulfilled (a hideous picture purged quickly from my mind), or the winning of a lottery. Whatever the case,

I departed before her mood darkened to its normal black hue.

So Danny and Johnny stayed in the classroom to work on their diorama once a week, with my door always open and other teachers on the floor. The two of them provided me with something every real teacher desires - polite, enthusiastic students so intensely interested in what they are teaching that they are willing to give up their free time to learn more. And it wasn't that they were strange and shunned by the other students. They were both pretty popular and had plenty of friends. I enjoyed watching them together as it brought back happy memories of the times spent with my own friends when I was in middle school. This was teacher heaven, at least for a while. Any situation that seems too good to be true usually is, and I was too new and naïve a teacher to visualize the trouble that could come from it in the future.

I still had my extra help classes once a week before a test, and any student was welcome, provided they had a note of permission from their parents. One day, Danny couldn't find the note from his mother (99.9 percent of notes from home were from mothers) in his backpack. He panicked, so I told him not to worry. We would go to the office during the lunch break and he could call his mother to fax the note to the school. Danny's mother was always in the school helping out with book sales, boutiques, and pizza days. If any parent deserved a small favor, it was her.

Unfortunately, when we arrived at the office, we ran into a big, fat roadblock in the form of Mrs. Devilica, whose scowl showed she was in the foulest of moods.

"Danny needs to call his mother. He can't find her note giving him permission to stay after school for extra help today," I said politely.

"That's too bad," she bellowed. "He's not tying up my telephone and fax machine. And you," she said to me with a mean smirk, "call his mother and tell her to pick him up at two-thirty."

Exerting monumental control to suppress an overwhelming impulse to point out truthful observations on her character, beginning with "miserable bitch," I managed to get Danny, who was visibly upset, out of that office fast. We went to the nurse's office and she, distracted by taking care of some student with a stomach ache, let me use her phone.

"Hello Mrs. Conti. I was told to call you by Mrs. Devilica. Danny can't find his note to stay after school and Mrs. Devilica said that you'll have to pick him up at two-thirty."

"I'll call the office and get it straightened out," she assured me. Which is exactly what she did, and

Danny stayed that night for help despite all the nonsense.

But the incident made me well aware that in dealing with Mrs. Devilica's nastiness, I was hanging onto self-control by my fingernails. It was only a matter of time before I slipped.

We had just finished the story of Samson and Delilah, the sixth-grade students enjoying the part when Samson pushes on the pillars in the temple and destroys it with all the Philistines inside. Anthony, a smart boy with a quick mind and a mischievous sense of humor, raised his hand.

"Yes, Anthony," I said, always happy to have a student show interest in what they just learned.

"So, all of Samson's strength was in his hair, and when Delilah hacked it off, he lost his strength?" he asked with a smirk.

"So the story goes."

"What about his pubic hair?" he said laughing.

My first impulse was to blurt out some flippant response like, "There wouldn't be enough strength in that to pull down a dollhouse." Or, worse still, "That strength Delilah wanted saved for herself." But I caught myself in time, aware that the age of my audience was twelve, not twenty. I knew that I should have been shocked and infuriated. Actually, I was neither, but I could pretend to be, as it made me feel more Catholic school teacher-like.

"We don't talk like that here," I said sternly, thinking that was a proper response. Fortunately, at that moment Carol came into the room and rescued Anthony from future reprimands.

"Mrs. Devilica sent me up to ask if you are going to help chaperone the dance this Friday night?" she asked, spotting her son at his desk, which abutted my own, and smiling in a mommy way.

"Sure, I'll be there," I responded, reasoning that, as a new teacher, it was a good idea to participate in as many events as possible. I smirked as I thought of the first dance I had attended at a Catholic School when I was thirteen.

"What's so amusing?" Carol asked.

"My first boy and girl dance was at a Catholic school was when I was thirteen. It was in a gym with the smiling girls lined up against one wall and the nervous boys lined up against the far wall across from them. The two giggling groups were separated by the no-man's land gulf of the gym floor. Leaning along another wall was a collection of brooms. When the music began, if you wanted to dance, you had to pick one the brooms as a partner and dance with that."

"You really weren't allowed to dance with each other?" she asked incredulously, her puzzled eyes showing Carol's mind was trying to conjure up the silly sight.

"That's right."

"Well, when I think of some of the dancing partners I've had over the years, a broom doesn't seem all that bad. Anyway, there won't be any brooms at the dance this Friday night, or," she lowered her voice so that it came to only my ears, "the witch that rides on one. Mrs. Devilica won't be there, so it should be fun."

"Aw shucks, and I wanted to waltz with her," I said sarcastically. Carol left the room shaking her head and laughing.

That dance! I shuttered every time I thought of it afterward, silently vowing never to chaperone one ever again. Yet it began innocently enough. When I arrived at the school a few minutes after seven that Friday night, the sixth, seventh, and eighth graders were already standing around in groups on the dance floor while the parents and teachers who had showed up to help were sitting in chairs near the refreshments. I spotted Danny's and Johnny's mothers and, strolling over to them, exchanged the usual teacher-parent pleasantries.

Carol came over from the direction of the office. She whispered mysteriously into Marge's ear, who nodded and walked over to the office. Then Carol motioned me over.

"Don't tell anyone, but we've got a bottle of vodka in the office, and if you want a drink, just follow Marge. She's going to have one now and she'll make you one," she said, giggling.

At first, I was too stunned to say anything and just stood there staring at her. For some strange reason, I thought that sneaking booze into a school dance was a risky rite-of-passage reserved for students, not the faculty members in charge of the event! So, I just smiled and politely declined.

"Well, just in case you want one later, the bottle is in the cabinet where the copy paper is stored," she added cheerfully.

The news of the staff drinking from the bottle of vodka was bad enough, but the behavior influenced by the trips to the office, and the late arrival of Marlene and her boyfriend, Bobby, after downing martinis at a local bar, was about to do away with any dignified behavior still left at the dance.

Marlene's vivacious demeanor at her arrival was a surprise to anyone who saw her previously in the school, with her sour face and dour dowager disposition. Here, she entered wiggling, giggling, and hanging onto the arm of her boyfriend with a "see what I caught" expression on her face. Both looked, and were, "three sheets to the wind." Carol came over to her, informed her about the hidden hoard of alcohol, and the two of them took off for the office, momentarily abandoning the boyfriend to the conversation of the class mothers.

Bobby wasted no time taking advantage of the situation and began blatantly flirting with them.

After all, they were young and attractive, and perhaps in his drunken daze he saw an opportunity. The mothers were not amused, so after a few moments he wandered outside.

By now the music was blasting and the students were doing what I supposed was a dance. They stood together and sort of jumped up and down. Marlene reappeared and, with her impaired mind reacting to an instructional impulse, decided to teach them a few steps. Smiling from ear to ear, she meandered over to the dancing area and began flailing her flabby arms, rolling her big head, and shaking her hundred-pound booty with total abandon. In shock, the students stared with "what the....?" expressions on their faces. Then, their manners pushed beyond the breaking point, they began laughing hysterically.

Marlene, in her happy haze, didn't even notice them and wildly twisted from side to side, looking like an overloaded and unbalanced washing machine. Watching her made me want to run to the bathroom. Instead, I fled outside for some much-needed fresh air and change of scenery. There in the cool, crystal clear moonlight I saw Bobby hiding behind the Mother Elizabeth Ann Seton statue drawing deeply on what appeared to be a joint. My mouth dropped open in horror and, not wanting to be spotted, much less asked to join him for a toke, I snuck back into the building.

The dance was beginning to take on the surrealism of a Fellini film, and I had a burning desire to depart before I became associated with any of the career-destroying nonsense. But before I could plead a medical misery and make a run for it, Mattie, the girl in my homeroom that Marge had attacked in the hallway, decided to do a close and grinding dance with an eighth-grade boy, leaving no room, as the nuns used to say, for the Holy Ghost between them. Marge spotted them and raced across the floor in a wild rage. Screaming, she grabbed their arms and flung them apart, twisting Mattie's arm in the process.

Mattie angrily stormed off to the girls' room, and I could picture in my mind the ugly consequences for Marge when Mattie's mother learned of the latest attack on her daughter. Having witnessed more than enough nonsense for one night, and not wanting my name or face forever associated with drunken teachers, illegal drugs, and student assault, I decided it was high time to depart. I quietly ducked out the door without looking back on such a sinful scene, fearing being turned into a pillar of salt.

On the ride home, I sorted through the sad sights of the past two hours and tried to make some sense out of them. As a kid, I loved the Superman comics that featured the Bizarro World, where everything was the exact opposite of what it should be. It seemed I had just viewed that world in real life. Wasn't it the students that were supposed to smuggle alcohol into a school function for a forbidden thrill? My friends in high school did that once, got caught, and were duly suspended. What spared me from sharing their sad fate was a stomach virus that kept me from going to that dance in the school gym. Then there was the class trip where we took a hypodermic needle from a friend's parent, who happened to be a doctor, and shot vodka into the oranges we placed in our lunch bags. One deceived chaperone on the trip remarked that they were happy to see we brought along healthy snacks. Best class trip ever!

Yet while this type of student behavior isn't exactly something to be proud of, it can be dismissed with the "what can you expect from crazy teenagers?" contempt it deserves. There is no cute excuse that teachers, tossing back drinks while chaperoning a school dance, can fall back on. And such hypocrites! Both Marge and Marlene were so fast to find fault with me. Meanwhile, they were both big boozers who were acting out on every neurotic impulse, giving no consideration to the consequence.

And what about Carol? Her behavior was the saddest surprise because, while I couldn't have cared less if Marge and Marlene suddenly vanished from the face of the earth, I held both Carol and her son in high regard. On the long, dark ride home, Shakespeare's phrase, "Lilies that fester smell far worse than weeds," suddenly came to mind, and the meaning became crystal clear.

By the time I pulled into the driveway, I had reached the conclusion that the school was somehow under a dread enchantment and probably needed a good exorcism. When the students misbehaved in my catechism class eons ago, stern Sister Catherine used to make us put our heads down on our desks. Then she strolled silently up and down the aisles, sprinkling holy water on our heads to rid us of the demonic possession that had somehow entered our little bodies and brains, forcing us to misbehave.

During an uneasy sleep that night, I dreamt that Marge, Marlene, Carol, and Mrs. Devilica were seated at the little desks in the first-grade classroom, heads down, while Sister Agnes, who taught that class, gleefully sprinkled holy water on the first three, then dumped a bucket of it on the fourth.

The next morning, while still in bed and stupid with sleep, I received an early call from Marge, who must have woken with a prayer to St. Bibiana on her lips.

"Could you believe Marlene and her boyfriend last night?" she gasped, making no mention, of course, of her own bad behavior.

"They both came to the dance dead drunk, and he was trying to carry on with the mothers there. I've never seen the like of it!"

It was easy to see right off what the purpose of her seemingly friendly call was. She was burning to find out how much I knew of last night's career-ending activities and who, if anyone, I would spill the beans to. I acted coyly, and, like many people desperately seeking information, she ended up giving away more than she gained.

"Carol told me that there was a bottle of vodka in the office, and I saw Marlene go in there with her to get a drink," I said with mysterious importance.

The silence was deafening on the other end of the line as Marge digested this information and tried to decide how to respond. Tossing Christian charity out the window, I smiled at the picture of her squirming while wondering if I had witnessed any of her shenanigans.

"I'm going to have to call Mrs. Devilica and tell her what went on," I threatened. "It's only right. I didn't do anything wrong and I don't want to be involved in what went on, so I'll tell her Monday morning before one of the mothers who were at the dance do."

I half expected to hear Marge fall to the floor with a heart seizure, but, despite the agony I was sure she was in, she managed admirable self-control.

"Well, you do what you have to do. I'm just glad I didn't do anything wrong," she said shortly, leaving me wondering irrelevantly if her statement was a mortal or venial sin.

Mrs. Devilica had said that we could call her at home if it concerned an important matter. Although she held the distinction of being the absolute last person in the world I wanted to talk to during a weekend, I called her on Sunday and left a message for her to call me back. She didn't. She dismissed my call with the same contempt as she did with everything connected with me. How different the rest of the school year would have played out if she hadn't.

I arrived at the school on Monday at the unheard-of hour of six in the morning. The plan books had to be handed in first thing in the morning and I had forgotten to bring mine home over the weekend to work on. Every class for every day had to be given an objective and means of meeting it. It was a total waste of time and I had come to the conclusion that whoever conceived of it was entitled to some extended sessions with the Inquisition.

I filled in the boxes representing the different days of the week impatiently, knowing Mrs. Devilica would invariably find fault with every line written and scribble nasty comments. When I had just finished the box for the Thursday seventh-grade religion class, writing about students learning the meaning of the Beatitude "Blessed are the merciful for they shall obtain mercy," the door opened, and a flushed and frightened Carol ran in.

"Jimmy," she cried, "Marge called me yesterday and said you were going to tell Mrs. Devilica about the drinking at the dance."

"Damn Marge," I thought, violently jamming my pen down on the Beatitude box. I had no intention of "telling" on Carol, only on the other two.

"I wasn't going to mention you," I assured her.

"But Marge and Marlene will. I know they will. They're not going to take the blame themselves," she wailed, her eyes burning with tears of fright. "Jimmy, please don't do it. Don't let me go out like this. I made a terrible mistake. I don't know why I did it. What about Michael? You can't do this to my son."

Sweet are the uses of motherhood. Of course I couldn't do that to her son, or to her, for that matter. Torn between a raging desire to rat out Marge and Marlene while, at the same time, wanting to protect Carol and Michael, I felt like an old cartoon character that had a little devil and angel whispering in his opposite ears during an internal struggle to do right or wrong. One long look at Carol, her face haggard with remorse and her arms apart, palms up in the age-old gesture of appeal, settled the matter. All that was missing from the scene was the ringing bell and three mea culpas. The little angel won, wings down.

"I won't say anything. I promise," I said reassuringly. "You're one of the few people here who have been good to me. I couldn't do that to you, or to Michael."

"Thank you, Jimmy," she said softly, smiling at me through sparkling tears. "Thank you."

Then she whipped her eyes dry, attempted to arrange her face into a look of casual nonchalance, and left for the office.

A half hour later I went down to hand in my plan book. Carol was at the copying machine and Mrs. Devilica was looking intently at the new weekly list of lunch specials from the local deli. Her eyes were dilated as she contemplated what to devour that day. She glanced up from the menu, spotted me, and then quickly looked back to the food choices.

"You called me over the weekend," said Mrs. Devilica in a tone implying I had committed a heinous crime. "I didn't have a chance to get back. What was it you wanted?"

Carol stood frozen in fear, despite my promise. Then she continued her task of making copies while I answered.

"I just had a question about the plan book, but I figured it out," I replied, taking fliers out of my box that were reminders to the students to bring in their two dollars for pizza day.

"Oh," she said with no interest. Then she brightened a bit and belted out, "Carol, call the deli later and tell them to send over a veal parmigiana wedge for my lunch."

Although I didn't tell on Marge, she still wasn't off the hook for her bad behavior at the dance. Her alcohol-fueled attack on Mattie had sent Mattie's mother on the warpath and after Marge's scalp. A few minutes after I left the office that Monday morning, she entered screaming. That afternoon after dismissal, I was correcting tests, listening to my Bessie Smith CD, wondering for the hundredth time why some students were too lazy to even fill in multiple choice answers, when a disheveled, terror-stricken Marge came into my room and sank down at one of the student's seats.

"Mattie's mother has threatened to have me investigated," Marge said morosely. "She said that she wants to sue the school. And all because I was trying to keep her daughter out of trouble."

I wanted to ask her what kind of trouble she thought Mattie was going to get into, as her close dance was in full view of dozens of other people, but I tactfully decided to remain silent. Somehow, I couldn't muster a spark of sympathy for Marge. She deserved whatever was coming to her. Nor would I champion her cause if summoned to the office to tell what I saw.

Bessie Smith began to belt out "*I'm sitting in the jailhouse now*," which seemed a perfect backdrop for Marge's concerns, and probably did little to lift her spirits.

"Well, I wish you luck," I replied, telling an officious lie. "Mattie's a pain in the neck and her mother's crazy," I continued, this time truthfully. "And by the way, you're sitting in Mattie's chair."

Once again, Marge lucked out. The whole incident was hushed up. Money talks, especially hush money, and Mattie probably ended up with free tuition for the duration of her stay in the school, if she hadn't received that treat from her earlier altercation with Marge. No one mentioned the dance again, but the fact that I knew what went on sat ill upon Marge and Marlene. Instead of deep thankfulness that I covered up their career-killing behavior, they resented me all the more and were cordial, but cool, from then on.

When Thanksgiving approached, I decided to have some students dress up as Pilgrims and Indians and go around to the other classrooms to give a little speech on the history of the holiday. The Pilgrim outfits were Halloween costumes I purchased cheaply at a leftover sale, and a reenacting friend who had made an Indian costume for her daughter years earlier loaned the costume to me. The closest thing I could find to use as a turkey was a rubber chicken. It was placed on a platter surrounded by sweet potatoes in a vain attempt at realism. The traveling Thanksgiving show was a smashing success, probably due to the fact there was some ad-libbing to my serious script. Teachers whose classrooms were visited reported to me that, on the way out of each room, the Pilgrim would attack the Indian with the rubber chicken while the Indian beat the chicken with a rubber tom-tom.

As I was packing away the costumes at the end of the day, Carol, on one of her frequent escapes from the office on some pretense, walked in. She had been the soul of appreciation since my decision to keep her behavior at the dance a secret, and she couldn't do enough for me as far as making copies in the office and calling parents. Spotting the Indian costume lying on a desk, she picked it up and, smiling, held it against her body.

"Would you mind if I borrowed it?" she asked, looking down to see the height of the hem.

"I think it will fit, and I want to play a joke on my husband. He's very interested in Native American culture. Once, he took Michael and I to some pow-wow or something. Whatever the hell it was, I was bored to death."

"It's all yours," I replied, amused by her silly request. "Here, take the hair, too." I tossed her the black wig with long braids made of wool. "Somehow your blond hair clashes with the costume."

"Thanks. This is great. My husband is going to love it," she said gratefully, rolling up the costume and placing the silly wig on top.

"Well, don't let him love it too much. I have to get it back to my friend and I'll be seeing her next weekend."

"Don't worry, I'll bring it back Monday," she assured me, contemplating the costume with a sly smile on her face.

"I hope you know that Indians didn't kiss. They hugged and sniffed one another," I said, not being able to stifle the childish impulse to gross her out. "And make sure you smear yourself with bear grease to be authentic."

"Ugh! That's disgusting," she said, giving me the same contorted facial reaction I received from my students when provided with the same information. Then Carol spotted the rubber tom-tom on a desk, took it to accessorize her outfit, and, with an Indian war whoop, went out the door contemplating the bedevilment of her husband. Some people never grow up, I thought, shaking my head. Then I went to my desk and rearranged the Thanksgiving display of Pilgrim, Indian, and turkey rubber duckies.

The next day was my turn to do yard duty. Cold weather had set in weeks earlier and it would only be a matter of time before the students would be spending much of their recess time indoors. Fine with me, as the novelty of having outside yard duty in the parking lot had worn off months ago. Fear of lawsuits had caused ball games to be forbidden, so most of the kids just walked around in a large circle, giving the place, appropriately enough, the appearance of a prison yard. The "unpopular" students, who were shunned by their classmates, talked to me as I supervised the behavior in the lot. Feeling sympathy for their situation, I always listened solicitously and made much of them.

The front door of the school opened and a coatless Carol sped across the lot to where I stood.

"Mrs. Devilica was watching you from the office window and she doesn't want you talking to the students when you have yard duty," she said in a low voice that, with all the screaming in the lot, barely reached my ears. "She sent me out here to tell you. I'm sorry. You know what she's like."

"Only too well," I whispered back, and then, to the students, "All right, you'll have to go and play with the other kids." Feeling rejected, they sadly and slowly wandered off.

"Did your husband like the Indian outfit?" I asked, attempting to diffuse my annoyance by changing the topic.

"He liked it all right," she replied, shivering slightly in the cold wind. "I'll try to bring it back tomorrow." She smiled and looked away, suddenly shy, and I tried to erase the image of Carol and her husband playing "two in the teepee."

"I'd better get in, I'm freezing. I'll bring the costume back tomorrow," she promised, running back to the building.

I didn't get the outfit back until that Friday. Fortunately, Carol was considerate enough to have washed it. Remembering the lines of a cowboy and Indian love song, *"Her black hair glistened in the silvery moonlight, you will always be my Rose of Cherokee,"* I wondered if Carol had to wear the wool wig and bang on the tom-tom while they had their teepee trysts, but I tactfully didn't ask.

The Christmas season came on quickly and, in a Catholic school, it is, for obvious reasons, celebrated in a big way. I looked forward to enjoying the season and the school activities that went along with it. My homeroom was picked to perform First Friday Mass. The week after the Mass, the Christmas play would be put on for the parents, followed by the classroom party and, best of all, Christmas vacation. But I should have been more guarded in my expectations after having spent three months in the school. Everything started off nicely, then went downhill as rapidly as a red sleigh on a steep, icy slope. Instead of a Santa-filled season to be jolly, it took a sustained effort not to become a snarling green Grinch.

As it was the first Mass I was in charge of, my mentor, Marge, was commanded by Mrs. Devilica to help me. She picked out the readings and the partitions and I chose students with good speaking voices to present them. Two days before the Mass, we went to the church and I scattered the thirty students in my homeroom throughout, one per pew, so that talking would be difficult at best. Then the students picked to do the Mass went up to the altar, which was now adorned with a plastic Jesse tree, whose tired and faded felt decorations appeared to be relics of a religious art project from decades ago. Everything went smoothly; we were ready for Friday.

As I entered the office to sign in the next morning, I noticed a piece of paper in my box. I knew by now that this was never a good sign, as it was usually a note from Mrs. Devilica with a criticism of past performance or a demand for a task to be done within an impossible time frame. My foreboding proved correct, as the note said that she didn't want a Christmas Mass but an Advent one. Everything had to be changed today and the Mass retyped and resubmitted to her. I cursed her silently as I charged up the stairs and into Marge's room.

"That bitch!" she cried. "After all that work. And I thought that it was beautifully done. I haven't got time to do it over."

I gave her one long look that conveyed my knowledge of her behavior at the dance and she suddenly softened her stance.

"I'll get it done by the end of the day. You'll have to take the class into the church and practice it first thing tomorrow morning before the Mass," she said shortly and I quickly left before she changed her mind.

After taking attendance the next morning, I lined the class up and we sped down to the church. We had exactly a half hour to rehearse before the Mass began. I was in no mood for nonsense and the students sensed it and behaved accordingly. The rehearsal was done with ten minutes to spare. Father Flattery, already decked out in his cosset, breezed in and took the revised prayer service. Then, to my horror, he asked one of the students for a pen and started to cross out items and make notes.

"That's much better," he announced, handing me back the prayer service paper and then disappearing into the back room. I looked at the paper and saw a collection of crossed out and rearranged homilies and gospels and the addition of something called antiphons. The entire service was an unrecognizable mess.

I wanted to curse God and die. I remembered someone in the Bible had wanted to do that, and now

I knew just how he felt. We had only ten minutes left before the Mass. Then I got an idea.

Johnny, one of the students who had spent some recesses in my room working on history projects, once told me that he had been an altar server for years. I figured that he must know everything about the workings of a Mass, so I made him an offer he couldn't refuse.

"Do you know what all this means?" I asked, apprehension written all over my face. He studied it closely for a moment and, to my vast relief, responded, "Yes."

"Listen, I really need your help," I said earnestly, looking him straight in the eyes. "Explain these changes to the others and rehearse them. I'll make you Student of the Month," I promised, wondering briefly if it was a sin to bribe a student, yet not caring if it was.

Johnny turned and began pointing and telling the other students involved in the Mass where to be and what to say with the expertise of a seasoned stage director.

"O Emmanuel, God with us, our king and lawgiver, the savior of nations, come and set us free!" said Sandy into a lowered microphone, completing the rushed rehearsal just as the first grade entered the church, their teacher facing them while holding a finger to her mouth.

Although I sweated out every reading, petition, and antiphon, and couldn't wait for the off-key singing of "Let there be Peace on Earth," the Mass went well. In gratitude, I brought Munchkins for the students the next day and Johnny received the promised Student of the Month for saving my… uh… the Mass and keeping me from breaking the second commandment with a chain of curses.

The eclectic Christmas decorations on my desk consisted of my version of a 1950s-style tree and an old Crèche I had picked off the ground at a flea market. The tree had bubble lights and ornaments of a '57 Chevy, *I Love Lucy*, Marilyn Monroe, and others of the same vein. On the window sill above the heating vents, the drooping candles in the Advent wreath stood next to a Santa flamingo that danced to the tune of "Jingle Bells." The students were enthralled.

"There's a list on the table in the teacher's lounge and you have to write what your class is going to do for the Christmas show," said Marge on the way back to her classroom after coming from lunch in the lounge. "I just wanted you to be aware of it because I know you never go in there," she continued with a slight contempt in her tone, then left to get ready to pick up her class from recess. I followed her, realizing she was right. I rarely had lunch with the other teachers and there were several reasons why. All they did in there was complain about the students, parents, and principal. One young teacher was getting married in the spring and talked about nothing but her upcoming wedding. It was beyond boring and a total waste of my limited time to be in that lounge and, after the first week of school, I rarely made an appearance, which made me a main item on the lunchtime gossip agenda.

"How would you like to sing 'Santa Claus is Coming to Town?'" I asked my homeroom. It was the end of the day and they were seated at their desks, waiting for prayers and then blessed dismissal. The question was rhetorical, as they were going have to sing it whether they liked it or not. By the time I viewed the list, most other popular Christmas tunes were already taken.

"We can have some of you decorating a Christmas tree as you sing, and near the end of the song, Santa and his elves can come out from the side of the stage and deliver oversized report cards with big A's on them," I added, trying to make the choice more enticing.

"I think Tony should be Santa," suggested Vanessa, recommending the largest and most easy-going boy in the class. Then everyone wanted to be an elf, or someone decorating the tree, or Rudolph, and I promised recklessly from left to right that they could. There was certainly no lack of enthusiasm.

"Mr. Consorte, why is there a dead spider on top of one of the wise men's heads?" asked Danny, distracted by what was indeed a large dead spider that had, in all probability, expired before I brought the Crèche.

The class, of course, screamed in unison.

"It's there to make the scene more realistic. The Holy Land was infested with spiders back then," I said, feeling that it sounded feasible, then quickly adding "Everyone stand. It's time for prayers."

"Should we pray for the poor again today?" asked Andrew, whom I had assigned as prayer leader for the week.

"No. They've got enough of our prayers for one week," I said selfishly. "Let's pray that our Christmas act goes well."

So, some of the class prayed a petition while, as usual, most went through the motions while their minds drifted off to a warming vision of the next fun event in their lives. I fervently hoped that the select amount of sincere prayers would be answered and God would somehow work a miracle just for our benefit. But, after the show, there was no need for a class prayer of gratitude.

Marge, a Dunkin' Donuts coffee in hand, raced into my room early the next morning, looking more than a little tired.

"Your stupid Steven entered my classroom yesterday afternoon like this," she spit out. Then, putting down the coffee, she pranced about and swung her arms in imitation.

Steven was the student who held the dubious honor of being the first one who had the nun doll on his desk due to his demented behavior. A serious attention addict, there wasn't much he wouldn't do if he thought that he had an interested audience. The nun doll had darkened his desk numerous times.

"I told him in front of your class to cut it out, that he looked like a gay reindeer," she confessed. "I didn't sleep at all last night worrying that Steven or one of the other kids would go home and tell their parents and I'd get into trouble again. But I couldn't help it. He looked like an old queen," she spit out in disgust.

"What next?" I thought, staring up at her haggard face. No one ever seemed to enter my room with any good news. They were either seeking sympathy or calling me down to the office to be scorched with hot words by a sufferer of flaming middle-age flashes.

"I'm sure Steven forgot all about it," I said reassuringly. "He's used to being reprimanded. Plus, you gave him what he wants, attention." Then, to change the subject, "Your class is doing the Nativity for the Christmas show, aren't you?"

"Yes. Can you picture that crew dressed in sheets and towels?" she said giggling, now in a good humor.

"And can you guess who wants to portray the Virgin Mary?" she asked, smirking.

"Who?"

"Amanda!" she cried, laughing. "The class whore is going to be the Virgin. Talk about casting against type!"

I laughed along with her, disregarding the fact that we were being as unprofessional as possible. Amanda was completely boy crazy and mature beyond her years. Some of the boys' mothers had actually called Marge to complain that their sons couldn't study because she was calling them ten times a night. She had been in trouble for grabbing a boy's butt as he bent over the water fountain, and the mother of a younger girl had complained to Mrs. Devilica that Amanda had explained to her daughter how to "do it." Portraying Mary Magdalene would have been a more appropriate role.

"And you should see the doll we have to use for the baby Jesus. It's an old Betsy Wetsy that must have been here since the 1950s. And it's missing a leg!" she cried, crowing with laughter. It was nice to share a lighthearted moment with her, and I wondered why she could not always be like this.

Marge wandered off to her classroom smiling, and a moment later I heard the usual morning screeching protest of metal as she lined up the students' desks.

Her tossing and turning with worry the previous evening was for nothing, as there were no noted complaints about Steven being called a gay reindeer. Our assessment of Amanda, unfortunately, proved all too true. The fruit was there to be eaten, she did not mean it to rot, and in the ninth grade she went from adoring a still, one-legged Betsy Wetsy on stage to attending to the screams of her own real, wiggling baby.

"Can the girls decorating the tree wear red pajamas?" asked Ashley.

We were discussing what the class would wear on stage for the Christmas show. Jeans were strictly forbidden, and everyone had to wear something red, white, or green. Up to this point, the rehearsals had been pitiful, and I figured at least the production should look good.

"I don't see why not, but they have to be full, modest pajamas," I responded, thinking that the red pajamas would lend a nice night before Christmas look.

"Can I wear white jeans?" questioned a girl who was obviously trying to evade my edict banning them.

"No," I said sternly. "No jeans of any color, period!"

"Can I wear my red sweatpants?" asked Adam.

"No, no sweatpants."

"I have a white sweatshirt that says Nike on it," announced Anthony. "Can I wear that?"

"No, nothing with advertising."

"Damn," I thought. Jeans, sweatshirts, sweatpants. What was the big deal for these kids to just dress nicely for one lousy night. I remembered the Christmas concerts I was in during my junior high days back in the Paleolithic Age. Shoes, dress slacks, white shirts and ties for boys, and dresses in winter tones for girls were de rigueur. We stood on the stage between two Christmas trees twinkling with lights and strained to reach the soaring notes in "Gloria" while glancing out over an audience of men in suits and women dressed to outdo one another. And now...

At least Tony, the student playing Santa, couldn't give me an argument. He would be in the costume I had from the years I played Santa for my friend's kids, and I didn't care if he wore a rapper's tee-shirt under it. Plus, he couldn't possible do a worse job than I did during my first stint as Santa. The plan was that after Christmas Eve dinner at my friend's home I was to disappear to the basement, get into the costume and, with a pillowcase full of dirty laundry slung over my shoulder, walk across the backyard waving and ho ho-ing as the happy parents and excited kids pointed and cheered from the living room window.

But sometimes even the best laid plans can go astray, especially if Santa had one too many eggnogs.

Once, after slipping on the snow crossing the back yard, I got hung up on an unexpected fence, with my red pants beginning to slide off as the children were quickly yanked away from the window. Hopefully, Tony's tenure as Santa would have a happier outcome.

A stop at a Dollar Store on my ride home from the school one frigid evening provided more props. Santa hats, reindeer antlers, elf ears, a box of cheap glass tree ornaments, and a cardboard fireplace were all purchased and hauled to the car. We were making headway with the rehearsals and the show was coming along nicely when, one morning before classes began, I received the inevitable dreaded call from the office.

"Mr. Consorte, please come down to the office before the students arrive."

"What did I do wrong now?" I thought as I raced down the stairs to be first amused and then aggravated.

I entered the office and viewed the incongruous sight of an angry Carol, clad in a red sweater with a Christmas wreath pin, standing next to the office Nativity, holding a chocolate penis on a stick wrapped in cellophane. A tradition at the school was Secret Santa, which consisted of picking names out of a hat and providing the person you secretly picked with a small gift in their box at the office during the weeks before Christmas. I had already received some assorted chocolate Santas and snowmen in mine. I assumed someone had been joking with Carol, a joke in somewhat questionable taste.

"I thought I would have a little fun and tease my Secret Santa person by putting this in their box, but Mrs. Devilica saw it and told me that it was entirely inappropriate for a Catholic school," she hissed in a low voice, keeping an eagle eye on Mrs. Devilica's closed door. "What am I supposed to do with it now?"

It was on the tip of my tongue to say, "Why not just eat it?" but I caught myself in time.

Nancy, the office manager, watched us while she placated some parent on the phone who was complaining about her daughter's less than stellar role in the fifth grade's Christmas act. Nancy had a run-in with a prissy priest earlier in the year when he made her son, Tommy, cry. Tommy had no longer wanted to be an altar server and Father Paul laid into him like a fury in an attempt to sell him a ticket on the Catholic guilt train. Nancy hadn't spoken to Father Paul since and would slip in belittling remarks about him when provided with any opportunity.

"Stick it in Father Paul's box!" she spit out viciously after hanging up the phone. "Although he would probably prefer white chocolate."

Carol and I couldn't help but laugh at her implication. We stopped instantly when Mrs. Devilica's office door swung open and a parent stepped out. Carol quickly moved behind the counter and stuck the chocolate penis in her pocketbook. The parent had just passed by us and out the door when Mrs. Devilica exploded.

"I heard that you told some of the girls they could wear pajamas for the Christmas show," she spat out, fixing me with a sharp eye.

"Yes, I did," I admitted. "They're going to be decorating a Christmas tree and they thought it would be cute to be in Christmas pajamas."

"It's not," she said adamantly. "Tell them when they come in that they can't wear the pajamas." Then she turned, picked up the "Specials of the Day" deli menu from the counter, and returned to her office to pick out a high-calorie listing.

Carol took the chocolate penis back out of her pocketbook and trust it up with one quick arm motion.

"My sentiments exactly," I said. Then, hearing the bell, I went out to bring my class in from the frosty parking lot.

Telling the students that they couldn't wear the pajamas was the last thing I wanted to do. Yesterday, the girls had brought the pajamas in to show one another their stage outfits. The pajamas looked like sexless clothing to be worn working in a rice paddy. It wasn't as if they were going to don teddies and slink around the stage singing "Santa Baby."

So, I told them to take up the issue with Mrs. Devilica, as she was the one, not me, denying them their enjoyment. I figured another black mark against her wouldn't make any difference, as they already despised her.

On the night of the show, it wouldn't have surprised me to see polar bears strolling down the sidewalk, it was that frigid. Parents and students were allowed into the school at seven o'clock. At ten minutes to seven, I looked out the window of my classroom and saw a number of early arrivals shivering outside the back door. Sympathizing with their discomfort, I went down and let them in. While they gratefully defrosted in the rear stairwell, I attempted a quick escape to my room, but was stopped dead by a scream from a version of Scrooge in the shape of a plum pudding.

"Mr. Consorte," yelled Mrs. Devilica from down the hall, "tell those people they have to wait outside!"

I refused to cast the parents and students out in the cold. After all, they were paying over five thousand dollars a year tuition to the school. They deserved ten minutes of heat, and, after Mrs. Devilica was distracted by Carol calling from the office, I snuck them up to my classroom and hid them there until the official time came and they could enter the auditorium.

The students, excited by the prospect of performing, were in my classroom getting into their costumes and either watching a DVD of *Pee-wee's Playhouse Christmas Special* or listening to my tape of *Crazy Christmas Tunes*. I had told them that they could bring in snacks and something to drink. After all, this was after hours, the classroom was far from the auditorium, and the door was closed so no one could hear us. So why not let them have a little fun?

I was going around the room attending to last minute emergencies, like taping up a broken antler on a reindeer hat and untying a knot in one of Santa's dirty sneakers, which was making it impossible to get it off so that he could get into his boots.

While I was struggling with the obstinate shoelace, perspiration beading my forehead, the door swung open and in barged Mrs. Devilica, panting as usual from climbing the steps. "I Want a Hippopotamus for Christmas" was playing on my tape player, which, unintentionally, was perfectly timed to announce her arrival. Mrs. Devilica's eyes swiftly scanned the room, and she started screaming.

"Mr. Consorte!" she screeched, her nostrils flaring like an attack animal. "One of the other teachers told me you were having a party. Stop this right now and make the students sit quietly at their desks until it's time for your class to go on!" Then she turned and stomped off, slamming the door behind her.

What we were having could hardly be called a party, and I wondered who had complained. There were only two candidates on that short list, each occupying a classroom next to mine, and neither was in any position to be casting stones.

Carol came up from the auditorium to call us to the stage as we were up next. The now nervous students lined up, quieted down, and, led by Santa, Rudolph, and a silly assortment of elves, paraded excitedly to the entrance of the stage. We were forced to wait while the sixth grade performed an interminable version of "The Twelve Days of Christmas." Finally, after what seemed like the twelve months of Christmas instead of days, the last discordant "partridge in a pear tree" chorus sounded, was duly applauded by a relieved audience now returned from its collective reverie, and the sixth graders exited stage right while we raced in from the left.

Props I had stored offstage, the Christmas tree on a table and a cardboard fireplace, were put in their proper spots, the students took their places, and we were set to go. Earlier, in the spirit of "the show must go on," I told the kids that no matter what happened, just continue. It was a good thing I did.

The act was to begin with two students entering carrying cookies and milk for Santa, placing them in front of the fireplace, then sitting down next to them.

Four girls (the ones who were supposed to be in pajamas) would start hanging the ornaments on the tree. All would start singing, and, on the last stanza, Rudolph, Santa, and the elves would enter and give out the giant-sized A+ report cards to the students in the front row. What could be cuter?

But our act proved, once again, that "the best laid plans of mice and men can go astray" as one disaster followed another in mounting panic, like the plagues of Egypt.

Kevin and Linda, the two students chosen to bring out the treats for Santa because they were short and looked like little kids, sat down in front of the fireplace, which instantly fell over on them. Scrambling to straighten it back up, they knocked over the milk and scattered the cookies across the stage. While this horror was happening, the students, who had no problem straining their vocal cords all year and never seeming to stop to draw a breath, suddenly got stage fright as soon as the curtain was drawn open and sang at the level of one decibel above silence.

I was in the wings making wild gestures at them to sing out. They raised their voices infinitesimally, to the point where they were now possibly audible to the first five rows. The girls decorating the tree put all the bulbs on one side, which caused the tree to topple over, smashing the glass bulbs in the process.

Some kid in the audience yelled out "timber," which caused an outbreak of quickly stifled laughter. The embarrassed decorators made a frantic but futile attempt to right the tree throughout the rest of the song, which, mercifully, was now nearing its end.

Any hope of the grand finale of Santa and entourage saving the show was shattered when I looked across the stage and saw the elf holding the report cards dropping them on the floor. At the same awful moment, one of the elves turned swiftly and knocked Ashley, our Rudolph, right in her red nose with his elbow. Her hand went instantly to her injury and she began crying hysterically.

By now, their cue to come out of the wings and deliver the report cards had come and gone. Finally, Ashley the reindeer, looking like she had been wounded by a hunter, staggered out with Santa and the elves behind her. Having not had the time to rearrange the report cards properly, half the ones they gave out were held up to the audience upside down.

After this final fiasco came polite, perfunctory applause, probably due to the vast relief of the audience that our misery was over. If any performance ever felt the wrath of God, it was our poor little Santa show. Perhaps if I had them sing something like "Oh Holy Night" or another selection having a more religious theme, heaven would have smiled on our efforts instead.

As the students left the stage, one of the boy elves turned to me and said, "We stunk, didn't we?" It was on the tip of my tongue to reply sarcastically, but seeing his woebegone expression, I softened and replied with a wane smile, "You did fine."

A few days before Christmas I decided to teach the students about different Christmas traditions.

"You can use the candy cane pens I gave you to take this test on the *History of Christmas* video," I said, counting the tests and handing them out as I passed each aisle. I had recorded the video from a television show and sensed that the students would enjoy it. As a precaution against their minds wandering while watching, I prepared a test with questions to be answered from the video. When the video proved to be such a success with the seventh grade, I showed it to the sixth and eighth graders, as well. Although the seventh grade seemed to be having trouble committing to memory the important dates from the Revolutionary War, they had no trouble remembering the information on Christmas, and I wished that the founding fathers had worn Santa caps instead of tricorns.

The last day of school before Christmas vacation should have been a cakewalk as it consisted of a classroom party in the morning and the teachers' luncheon in the afternoon. I arranged the classroom for the party, setting up a table against a wall for all the totally unhealthy treats the kids would bring in and then gobble up. On each student's desks I placed their gift from me, a Santa Pez dispenser. The tree lights were plugged in and my Phil Spector Christmas CD and I looked forward to watching the kids have a good time (I had a CD of The Sisters of Solace singing old Christmas songs but decided to spare the students).

The smiling, overly animated students arrived carrying shopping bags loaded with food for the party, and cards and gifts for me and their friends. I didn't expect anything like this. The entire front of the room was lined with my presents! The parents who purchased them must have known my situation at the school, as half of the gifts seemed to be bottles of booze. Everyone was eating, talking, taking pictures, and giving gifts. Then, in the middle of the juvenile merriment, a concerned looking Carol entered the room with news that was as welcome to me at this moment as a coal-stuffed stocking.

"Let me guess," I said, with a knowing smile, "Mrs. Devilica wants to see me and you're going to watch my class." Carol rolled her eyes and nodded.

"As usual, you're getting the best of the deal. Judging from the past, I don't think she just wants to wish me a merry Christmas. Have whatever you want to eat, but don't expect a gourmet feast," I said, gesturing toward the picked-over junk food on the table.

As Carol wandered over to snatch up the last cupcake with green icing and red sprinkles, I walked past the parties going on in every classroom. I couldn't imagine what I could have done wrong, but so far this school year had more than its share of surprises.

Mrs. Devilica, looking like a week-old Christmas plum pudding that had grown legs, was standing next to her desk when I walked in. She wasted no time lashing out at me.

"Marlene told me that you showed a Christmas tape to her sixth graders that said Jesus was born in the springtime, not on December 25th, and that you're confusing the students," she said, fixing me with a malevolent eye. "Marlene has her period and is very emotional today, so she is pretty upset about it."

That was far more information than I needed, or wanted, to know. Before I could respond to my accusation of being a heretic, the inquisition continued.

"I want you to go tell the students that Jesus was born on the 25th of December and that the video you showed them was wrong!" she commanded, looking like she was ready to apply the thumbscrews or break me on the wheel if I refused to recant my hideous heresy.

"Will all great Neptune's oceans wash this blood clean from my hands?" was my sardonic response, as I valiantly tried not to lose my temper over this stupid situation. I could tell that she expected me to be severely contrite, but I couldn't be apologetic over something that I didn't see as a serious problem.

"Can't this wait until after the holidays?" I questioned. "The students are in the middle of their parties and I'll look like an idiot going into their classrooms now and interrupting them with something like this."

"No!" she screamed. "Do it right now!"

With that, I turned on my heel and marched out of the office, hoping that my rage would somehow melt away before I reached the sixth-grade classroom. It would never do for the students to see me upset, especially today. I had become an apt pupil at hiding my emotions from the students, so something like a well-trained mask came down over my face as I walked through the doorway and was greeted with a cold look from a cramp-consumed Marlene.

"Could you please tell the students that I want to make an announcement?" I asked, smiling so that she wouldn't know I was upset.

"Hey, everyone, listen up," she yelled, trying to be heard over the noise of the celebration. "Mr. Consorte has an announcement to make."

"I just wanted to wish you all a merry Christmas and to let you know that the video we watched was wrong," I said to an audience straining to be quiet. "Jesus was born on December 25th, and that's why we celebrate his birthday that day. Enjoy your vacation," I finished, and departed quickly, feeling like a fool and knowing they were frantic to return to their festivities.

I repeated this same performance with the eighth grade and then my own class. Most of the eighth graders wouldn't have cared if Jesus suddenly rode into the room on a donkey, much less when he was born. My class paid me perfunctory courtesy while chewing on the chocolate snowmen recently passed out by Ashley. Fortunately, just as I began my apology, the parent portraying Santa came ho-hoing into the room to hand out the Secret Santa gifts, and my voice was drowned out by wild cheering, sparing me any more embarrassment. After Santa left and the students were comparing their newly acquired treasures, the continuation of my insincere apology conveniently slipped my mind.

A friend had given me a model of the Times Square building that played "Aude Lang Syne" as the ball descended as a Christmas gift last year. I turned it on as I led the kids out of the classroom and told them, "See you next year," while wondering if I would, because I sensed by now that I was on borrowed time in this building. Then I proceeded to clean up the classroom and take down the decorations until Marge came in, holding what looked like ceramic praying hands.

"God, I'm glad that's over," she said with an exaggerated sigh. "We're having a 'worst teacher Christmas gift' contest and I'm entering this awful thing Nancy gave me. It's probably been re-gifted." She held up the praying hands and made a face.

"If you want to be in the contest, just bring the worst gift you got from the students down to the office. Mrs. Devilica is the judge, and the winner receives a free Christmas lottery ticket to win a million dollars." Then she left for the office with her pious contest entry for worst gift.

Looking down at my dozens of gifts, I immediately eliminated the bottles and gift cards and began to open some of the boxes. The silk ties and sweaters from Old Navy weren't at all bad, and my search for something awful went unrewarded until I opened a box that contained a Santa riding on a Harley Davidson motorcycle. I pressed a button on the bottom and the cycle made revving-up noises and played "Born to be Wild." It was a sure winner, and I could barely wait to get it to the office. Then I read the card.

"Dear Mr. Consorte - You are the best teacher I've ever had in all the schools I've ever been to. I remember you telling the class that you used to have a

Harley Davidson motorcycle when you were younger. When I saw this in the store, I picked it out for you because I knew you would like it. I hope that you have a very merry Christmas. Your student, Eddie." The last two sentences were tough to decipher because they were read through a blur of tears.

Eddie was a special-ed student who, though he tried hard, never did very well on tests, and probably never would. He was always smiling, polite, and never caused any problems. His handpicked gift and the sincere emotion in his card showed a sensitivity for others rarely displayed by seventh graders.

Other cards from various gifts were in the same vein. It seemed that the crummier the gift, the more touching the card. I couldn't enter any of them in a "worst gift contest." The winner ended up being a ceramic soap dish with a green frog squatting on top, submitted by the fourth-grade teacher. The lottery ticket, appropriately, was a loser.

The thought of going to the luncheon after what I was put through that morning was abhorrent, but not going would have just caused more problems. I wanted to get to the restaurant early so that I could at least claim a seat by someone whose company could be enjoyed, but the cleaning of the classroom and loading of the car with Christmas gifts took a bit of time. As I tied up the garbage bags containing colorful wrapping paper and dirty plastic cups, I wished that I had worn my Renaissance-style ring with the secret compartment to hide poison, as I considered it the perfect attire for this party. When we studied that time period, the students were fascinated with the Borgias and their lovely way of dealing with rivals, so I brought the ring in to show them how it worked. Ashley borrowed it at lunchtime one time so she could pretend that she was poisoning her friends in the cafeteria. But if I wore the ring to the luncheon, I don't think I would want to pretend, so turning the other cheek was a safer option.

By the time I arrived at the restaurant, my choice of chairs was limited to a seat next to Mrs. Devilica (no surprise that it was vacant), or one between Carlos, the non-English speaking custodian, and seventy-year-old Sister Carol. I chose the latter, and although the conversation was extremely limited, it was much more congenial.

Christmas Eve found me at my friend Emily's home. She shared my Italian background, so the yard was crammed with kitschy decorations, the centerpiece being the manger with lighted plastic figures. What was missing was the baby Jesus, who would be placed in his straw crib at midnight and plugged in with great ceremony. Inside, the house smelled of frying flounder as the traditional feast of the seven fish was being prepared. The grandmothers and old aunts were relegated to the living room.

Seated around the tree, which was trimmed with headache inducing blinking lights, they pointed to necks and knees, loudly and demonstratively complaining of the aches and pains that were the unwelcome result of increasing age.

When I greeted them and announced that I was now a teacher in a Catholic school, I was quickly told several horror tales of their experiences as children at the hands of strict Sisters.

"I was left handed and the nun said it was a sign of the devil, so she used to stick my hand with a pin if she saw me writing with it," lamented Aunt Lucy, thrusting a molted and withered claw in my face. "When my father, bless his soul, saw my hand at the dinner table one night, he asked me what had happened to it, and I told him. He went to see the nun the next day. 'You no stick-a my daughter with the pin no more, she not the devil,' he told her. And, after that, the nun never did," she finished triumphantly.

In the spirit of sibling rivalry, her sister, Aunt Connie, forming her hands in a praying position, cried out, "They used to sprinkle rice on the floor, and if I was caught talking, I had to kneel in a praying position on the rice for an hour. Madonna, that hurt like hell!"

"Ah, that was nothing," said Aunt Lucy dismissively. "The pin in the hand was worse."

"You think so?" cried Aunt Connie. "I'll go get some rice from the kitchen and you can kneel on it for an hour and see how you feel," she threatened, trying to lift herself off the couch.

The conversation was getting into deep and stormy water when, fortunately, someone in the kitchen screamed "the fish is ready." The memories of yesteryear were quickly replaced with the tantalizing thoughts of baccala and calamari.

After dinner and a couple of cocktails, Emily, who was also a teacher, and I were discussing some of our less than sterling students, comparing their foibles and laughing. Her teenage son overheard us.

"I didn't think teachers talked like this about their students," he said, amazed and appalled.

"Well, now you know," said Emily, unfazed, "and it's usually worse. We're only being nice tonight because it's Christmas Eve." He shook his head and went off to the basement to happily celebrate the birth of his savior by playing a violent video game with his cousin while Emily and I joined the group in the living room, who were watching a tape of old *Andy Williams Christmas Special*s and talking about the few precious toys they received from Santa decades ago.

Chapter 8

It is the Winter of Our Discontent

We returned to work the day after the New Year started, and the school, now denuded of the holiday decorations and anticipation of festivities, seemed somewhat bleak and depressing. "How was your vacation?" was asked continuously to and by arriving teachers and staff, and the same pat response repeated- "Too short."

I went around the room putting the thirty thank you cards, which had taken me an entire afternoon to write, on the students' desks. For the first time since the beginning of the year, I was actually caught up. All the time consuming test, homework, and composition correcting was done. But I knew the breather would be brief, as the assignments and projects I had given out to be done over the vacation would soon be handed in, at least by those who had completed them, and I would soon have another pile of papers on my desk.

The sixth grade was about to begin studying the French Revolution, so I brought in my miniature guillotine and Marie Antoinette doll with an ejector head so that the students could enjoy beheading her. I was adjusting the plastic blade on the guillotine when Danny and his father walked in, proudly carrying a diorama they had made of Custer's Last Stand.

"It looks great," I cried, hoping to make them happy as they set down the diorama on a table and began pointing out the different features of the cardboard battlefield, including the plastic soldier glued to the ground who was supposed to be a shot General Custer. "You definitely get an A for the project."

They left the room, beaming with pride, while I set up a talking Martin Luther King picture on the wall next to a poster of Betty Hutton as Annie Oakley in preparation for both our next holiday and my "Famous Women of the Month in History" series.

If I were under any delusion that the new year would bring brighter days to my situation at the school, I was swiftly and sadly disappointed. In fact, the problems were about to increase exponentially. Some of the troubles were caused by, of all the things, basketball games. The boys on the school's team asked me to come and watch them play. I felt flattered and said "yes," even though it meant having to make the half-hour return to the school on icy evenings and then back home again to drop into bed exhausted.

I sat with the parents on folding chairs against the wall, as there were no bleachers. There wasn't a relaxing moment to be had when the game was in progress, as you ran a very real risk of being smashed in the face by a flying ball as you attempted to watch the game and chat with the parents. The problem was that I found I had a lot of interests in common with some of them and enjoyed their company. Still a new teacher, I was naïve not to know that being too chummy with parents could only lead to trouble. Once growing fond of them, you feel terrible not giving their kids a good grade. Plus, other parents and students feel slighted if they suspect favoritism in any form, unless, of course, their kids are receiving the lion's share of it. Much of the limited time that I had was now spent in non-paying tutoring sessions for students who would have done poorly otherwise due to their allergic reaction to homework and tests.

"Who can tell me one of the hardships people faced during the Civil War?" I asked the seventh-grade class, expecting to hear some excellent responses as we had covered that time period in great depth. Beside the run-of-the-mill reading of the textbook, we did many homework handouts, and the students made Civil War newspapers as a project. We also watched segments from movies and documentaries about the time period. To show them the styles and behavior of plantation society, we watched the scene in *Gone with the Wind* with Mammy dressing Miss Scarlett. She laces Miss Scarlett into a corset and demands that she can't wear a low-cut evening dress to a daytime party because she "can't show her bosom until three o'clock." We then learned of the generals, battles, and famous politicians, and even played Civil War bingo.

For fun, we even had a military court with one of the soldier students on trial for getting drunk and striking an officer who constantly picked on him. If convicted, the soldier was to be shot in the back with a big plastic cannon ball fired from my Johnny Reb Cannon.

Eric was picked to go on trial and, when I told his mother, Mary, who managed the school office, of her son's dire predicament, she gleefully insisted on coming up to the classroom if he was convicted and carrying out the death sentence herself by pulling the lanyard on the cannon. Of course, the class voted a guilty verdict, so Mary took aim and fired with unerring accuracy. Eric was hit in the middle of his back as his bloodthirsty classmates cheered.

So, with all the knowledge of the time period successfully transferred to my students, I eagerly awaited an intelligent reply to my question regarding the important facts from the war. Many hands shot up, including Charlie's, a quiet and shy student who never gave me a single problem. Because he rarely raised his hand and seemed so happy to know an answer, I quickly chose him.

"That you couldn't show cleavage until three o'clock," Charlie answered proudly, without a hint of wise-ass in his serious voice.

The students were still, as if struck dumb, for a second before suddenly bursting into well-justified and sustained laughter. Instead of being embarrassed, Charlie seemed pleased with the effect his unexpected answer elicited from the class and began to chuckle. I supposed that I should have been upset, or at least act as if I were upset, but I began laughing so hard I started chocking. The water fountain in the hall was just outside my classroom door, so I assumed ducking out for a fast drink wouldn't cause a problem. The adage "it's never safe to assume" was about to be proven correct once again.

As I slurped down the stream of water, staring at a hardened piece of pink gum some gross student had spit out, I concluded that to Charlie, at age thirteen, the propriety of having to wear a high neckline until three in the afternoon probably did seem like an extreme hardship for men, right on par with battlefield wounds and camp diseases. He probably wondered why the men bothered to even get out of bed until late in the afternoon, when the viewing could begin.

I raced back to the room, becoming somewhat concerned as the tide of laughter, instead of ebbing, seemed to be rapidly rising. Inside the room was a teacher's worst nightmare.

The temperature in the room always seemed to alternate between the freezer aisle of a supermarket and an equatorial rain forest. The heater had been blasting non-stop all day, slowly roasting the students. When one girl complained that her stockings were ready to go up in flames, I let her open the windows, and that's where I found the entire class when I entered the room. Quickly walking to the windows to see what was so amusing, I spotted a grim-faced Mrs. Devilica seated at the steering wheel of her van, which she had stupidly parked on dirt that had morphed into mud from the combination of some warm weather and melting snow. She kept gunning the engine, digging herself in deeper, as Jose, the janitor, located behind the van, was slipping and sliding as he made a determined but futile effort to push her out.

The scene made a great show for the students, who were laughing hysterically, giving no thought, as usual, to the consequences of their behavior. But their teacher knew only too well. The Lord may have said vengeance was His, but, in this case, it would be hers, and it wouldn't be limited to the kids.

"Close those windows and get back to your seats!" I screamed. They complied, sensing the extent of my anger. Just before the last window was slammed shut, Johnny insanely issued the final, infuriating insult by shouting, "She's so fat, that's why she got stuck in the mud!" I should have just walked to my car and headed for home, for I knew my life at the school wouldn't be worth living from then on.

After giving the class a well-deserved tongue lashing, I told them to open their religion books and begin reading the page on St. Simeon Salus, the patron saint of madness. Ashley asked to go to the girls' room and, as I had been advised not to refuse that request to girls past a certain age, I let her. Seconds later she flew back into the room, fear written all over her face.

"She's coming!" screamed the female Paul Revere. I wanted to leap out the window, and I'm sure the scared students would have followed like lemmings, but it was too late. Ashley reached the relative safety of her desk and, staring down at her textbook, attempted to assume a look of studied nonchalance. The rest of the class, almost frozen in fear, modeled themselves on her example, and the room soon looked like an important test was being given.

Because Mrs. Devilica walked with the speed and wobbling gait of a dying elephant making its way to the bone yard, we had to suffer some long, agonizing seconds before she burst into the room. The students were attacked first.

"How dare you?" she yelled, her face red with rage. "I want every one of you to copy word for word the first three chapters in the religion textbook this weekend and hand it in first thing Monday morning!" Then she swung on me like a duelist who, having withdrawn a sword from one wounded opponent, turns hungrily for another.

"And you, Mr. Consorte!" she snarled, meeting my eyes squarely. "Don't you have any control of your class? What kind of a teacher are you?"

By now my face was also red, but with suppressed anger at being, once again, berated and humiliated before my students. I managed by heroic control to keep my mouth shut and not make matters even worse than they already were.

As if by divine intervention, Carol's voice came over the PA system, announcing that Mrs. Devilica's lunch order had arrived from the deli. Casting one last dirty look at me, the sphere made a half rotation and began her slow orbit to the office, forced on by the gravitational pull of the promise of a veal parmigiana wedge. Before we could recover from her severe scolding, the bell rang and the students got ready to go to their science class. As they left the room, Danny came over to me and said, "She really hates you, doesn't she, Mr. Consorte? I can tell by the way she talks to you." That remark summed up the situation perfectly.

Once again, I wanted to walk out the door and leave the school forever, but I couldn't bring myself to do it. Despite everything that had occurred, I actually enjoyed teaching, and I came to the disturbing conclusion that I just might be a masochist. However, Mrs. Devilica held the proverbial hourglass over my head, and I knew the sands of my stay at the school were slowly but inexorably running down.

Chapter 9

Jesus' Kingdom of Love

The fear instilled in the seventh grade by Mrs. Devilica showed itself a short time later at the Feast of St. Blaise. The teachers had to take their classes to the church so the students could have their throats blessed, but first I had to give them some background information about the saint. After the boring part about when he was born, what he did for a living, and how, on his intercession, a child was healed of a throat ailment, we got to the good stuff.

"He was martyred by being beaten, attacked with iron carding combs, and beheaded," I announced to their morbid delight. "That's why he's the patron saint of throats. So if you get a fish bone stuck in your throat, pray to him pronto."

"What if that doesn't work?" asked Danny, his face displaying his honest concern.

"Then find someone to give you the Heimlich Maneuver," I replied.

"I don't eat fish anyway," he said, vastly relieved that he would never need to bother neither a saint nor a mere mortal to save him from the embarrassment of choking to death in front of his friends in the cafeteria.

"In Croatia," I continued, "they parade his head and a bit of bone from his throat through the town to celebrate his feast day. None of his body parts are here at the school, so all you get to do is have your throats blessed. Now line up and let's go."

The blessings were being performed in the gym by two priests and, to the shock and dismay of the students, Mrs. Devilica.

"I hope we don't get her," I overheard many of them nervously muttering as we stood waiting with the other assembled classes for the throat blessing show to begin. Then a nervous Johnny asked me the dreaded question.

"Mr. Consorte, we won't have to go to her, will we?"

"Probably not," I reassured him with a positive attitude I was far from feeling. "The odds are pretty good, one in three, that you won't. And it's no big deal anyway."

Then, as soon as the words were out of my mouth, Father Paul, in his less than divine wisdom, divided up the classes and announced: "The sixth, seventh, and eighth grades line up for Mrs. Devilica."

We lined up in front of the principal, who was solemnly holding what appeared to be two crossed, menacing looking sticks. Instantly, a stupid rumor spread through the ranks that she was holding nunchucks and was going to snap their necks. In abject terror, they all scrambled to be the last in line.

"Stop that now!" I hissed, scowling at them. "I'll go first to show you it's safe, and the rest of you follow." I could have added that, if there was any neck she wanted to snap, it was probably mine.

So, I received the first blessing, or, more probably, cursing, judging by the malignant, penetrating stare from Mrs. Devilica. I prayed devoutly that evening that I wouldn't be stricken with a throat tumor.

Actually, I had become pretty good at praying by now due to the Catechist Formation classes that Catholic school teachers were forced to take.

"You can find many times and places to pray throughout the day," said the short, middle-aged woman teaching a class called "Bringing Prayer Into Your Life and Classroom." You could tell by her detached, almost other-worldly expression that that she was really into her mission of spreading the good word. Or just spaced out on valium.

"I even pray when at the gas pumps while I'm pumping gas," she continued, and I pictured her face lifted to heaven while her hands held a hose, the amount of petrol purchased spinning on the pump. I decided to take her advice to heart and, the next time at the pump, I would pray for the price of gas to go down.

This same pious soul also regaled us with stories of her son's perfect family life, complete with the requisite wonderful wife and gifted children.

"I feel so blessed with my family," she sighed contentedly as she suggested ways to bring a religious atmosphere to our classrooms by setting up a prayer table displaying oil and candles, hopefully not setting the students or school on fire in the process.

At the next class I took with her, she was singing a very different tune. Her wonderful daughter-in-law had deserted her son for another man, taking the two children in tow.

"But I still pray for her, even though she ruined my son and his children's lives," she informed us, trying to assume a serene and forgiving stance. But her eyes showed that she was seething within and secretly desired to stone the erring woman.

Most of the courses were taught by priests, all seeming to be cast from the same mold. They were all smiles and chuckles as they taught their classes, adding many amusing anecdotes, which made the classes highly entertaining. But when the class would end, it was like a switch was flicked. All smiles and joking were done with, and they became very dismissive, as if you were now an annoyance. They would turn on their heels and run out the door, leaving you feeling disappointed and suspecting it had all been a well scripted-act.

A class called "Bring the Light to Your Students" was taught by a married teacher who had a multitude of children. Throughout the lesson, he was constantly interrupted by calls on his cell phone from a female student. He informed us that she had problems but, through his guidance, she had an epiphany and was now all smiles. It sounded so sweet, and I hoped for his family's sake the next step in the story didn't involve his epiphany during a stay in jail.

But I did learn a lot about religion, and I began to enjoy teaching it, although the most interesting tidbits had to be avoided. If students questioned the teachings in the Good Book, I told them that I am relating the teachings of the Catholic Church, many things defy logic, and belief in them is based on faith. That usually got me off the hook. If that failed, I told them to go ask Father Peter.

We eventually got to the chapter I dreaded entitled "Jesus' Kingdom of Love," which had little to do with either Jesus or love. A better title would have been, "Everything you always wanted to know about sex but will not learn about here," as it essentially taught that you couldn't "do" anything with anyone unless you were married, and, even then, you could only "do it" to have children. I prayed that this chapter would be over very quickly and with a very limited amount of questions, preferably none at all.

I had long ago gotten over the shock that my students' minds weren't as pure as the driven snow. Some notes that I had intercepted being passed around the classroom showed that. My favorite was the one that showed a cartoon format of Mrs. Devilica and me in bed together "doing it," complete with sound effects (ugh!) and her having a baby nine months later. The perpetrator showed very limited artistic skill at best, as Mrs. Devilica was drawn as a frowning snowman and I was portrayed as a smiling stickman, yet they were perceptive enough to capture the degree of warmth in her personality.

While reading a chapter from *My Brother Sam Is Dead* aloud in class, we came to the part where the sleeping teenage Sam has hidden the Brown Bess musket in the bed with him and his brother Tim tries to take it. "*I realized I was touching something funny,*" read Ashley innocently. "*I felt along the edge of the bed. There was something long and hard under the blanket.*" She blushed beet red as the class erupted into uncontrollable laughter. Trying to smooth over the awkward situation, I quickly took over the reading while overhearing one of the students say to another, "Instead of *My Brother Sam Is Dead,* the book should be titled *My Brother Sam Is Hot.*" I made a silent vow never to read that chapter aloud in class again, realizing that the students would turn almost anything into sexual connotations.

This was nothing new, and I could not condemn them, as my friends and I did the exact same nonsense in the seventh grade with our breezy boyhood banter. One seventh-grade associate, Gary, had a unique talent to turn the lyrics of every song that came out at the time into something "dirty" to entertain us in the school cafeteria. The Beatles' "*Close your eyes and I'll kiss you, tomorrow I'll miss you,*" became, "*Close your eyes, spread your legs, and I'll fertilize your eggs.*" He even tackled the lyrics in innocent nursery rhymes, his most creative being, "*Old Mother Hubbard went to the cupboard to get her dog Rover a bone. When she bent over, Rover took over, and gave her a bone of his own.*"

Gary's ability to produce sexual double entendres reached its zenith when he snuck into the science classroom at lunchtime and wrote his version of a chemical equation on the board: "The heat of the meat is directly proportional to the angle of the dangle." This great talent (great, at least, to a seventh grader) of gross rhyming granted Gary god-like status and a special seat at any of the "boys' tables" in the cafeteria. And with these memories in mind, it was time to tackle the dreaded "Kingdom of Love" chapter.

"*Each person faces the challenge of learning to control his or her sexual drive, otherwise the drive will begin to control the person. It is like riding a bike down a steep hill in the city and discovering the brakes do not work. The bike is taking you right into heavy traffic. You want to be in control of your thoughts, words, and actions,*" Andrew read with as straight a face as possible. I thought "so far so good" and quickly switched readers.

"*One way to keep your sexual drive in control is to participate in good activities such as sports, hobbies, or service,*" said Michael, smiling broadly, as I silently compared this advice to what good Catholic kids were told many masturbation sessions ago. When we felt a sexual urge coming on, we were instructed to fall to our knees and start praying fervently to the Blessed Virgin to make the sinful feelings go away. The next best thing was to start reading a book or perform some sort of heavy labor. If I remember correctly, neither of these offered a permanent solution to the "problem."

"*Using sex for purposes for which it was not intended is like playing with dynamite,*" Michael continued, still smiling, and I overheard from somewhere in the classroom, "They mean a stick of dynamite." Barely able to read at this point, Michael still managed to blurt out the final advice in the chapter, "*Sex should never be used for entertainment.*"

That pretty much brought down the house and, thank God, ended the chapter.

"Answer the question at the bottom of the page that reads, 'Why do you think young people have sex today?'" I commanded in an attempt to divert their attention and move on. "I'll come around and check your answers." Most of the answers followed stated basic truths, the girls saying that they wanted to keep their boyfriends and the boys revealing, hopefully not from experience, that it felt really, really good. I didn't question the answers.

Chapter 10

And Deliver Us from Evil

It was February and time for the yearly teachers' conference at a high school in a congested and gridlocked city neighborhood. We were told that parking would be severely limited at best, so some of the teachers, myself included, chipped-in and took a car service. The ones who tried to save a buck were condemned to what must have seemed like a version of the ninth circle of hell. They wasted an hour trying to find spaces on the street, only to later forget where they parked and wander aimlessly and in tears through a crummy area while attempting to locate their lost autos.

The first activity of the day involved free food, so everyone piled into the cafeteria for bagels, muffins, and coffee. Of course, we had to sit at the table with our principal and fellow teachers from the school. Everyone made sure their principals saw them so they would not be accused of playing hooky (which everyone would have loved to do) and get docked for the day. Then we all trooped into the auditorium for some inspirational speeches and the always requisite Mass. The older teachers, bred to politeness to their superiors, silently watched and properly responded while some of the younger teachers talked and sent e-mails.

Before the afternoon classes we were required to take, the crowd swarmed back into the cafeteria and lined up for lunch, some of the bigger and more brazen trying to cut the line. While walking over to get a place in the long line, I spotted Mr. Thomas, the principal from St. Dymphna's who had wanted to hire me the previous year. He was standing alone and, on an impulse, I swiftly headed for him.

"Hi, Mr. Thomas, remember me?" I asked with an ingratiating smile.

After shooting a startled look at me he replied warmly, "Hello, Jimmy. How is everything working out at Our Lady of The Holy Rosary Beads?"

"Not good, to be honest. It's been a pretty rough year," I admitted. "I remember that you wanted me last year. If you still want me, you can have me," I blurted out stupidly before realizing that it sounded almost sexual.

He stared at me, an inscrutable expression on his face, and I couldn't tell if he was still interested in employing me or just thought that I had suddenly taken leave of my senses. Then, after a few seconds of thought, he answered me.

"This is strictly between you and me," he said, with a very man-to-man attitude. "I know Mrs. Devilica's reputation. Almost her entire school quit last year. I had to let Mr. Foster go earlier this year for inappropriate behavior and now have a substitute who isn't working out very well either. The job is yours next year, but just don't mention this to anyone."

"I won't," I promised stoutly, smiling at my incredibly good fortune.

"Call me in June and we'll discuss the details then," he said, giving me my cue to take off as he turned to talk with another principal who wanted his attention.

"Too good to be true, too good to be true," sang my happy heart as I stood in the lunch line, eventually snatching a turkey sandwich and bottle of water. Sitting with the other teachers from my school at a table, I smirked, thinking that now I could deal with Mrs. Devilica's nastiness with equanimity. I must have looked like the proverbial cat that swallowed the canary.

During the dull, dreary days of March, the students and I were grateful to have a class trip. The destination was a local Catholic high school whose drama club was putting on a performance of the play *One Flew Over the Cuckoo's Nest*. I thought it

was an odd pick for seventh graders, but the title
did seem to sum-up my current daily experience,
and the character of Nurse Ratched bore a stunning
resemblance to Mrs. Devilica.

Problems began when more mothers wanted to go
as chaperones than there were available seats for them
on the bus. With the resulting bitching and charges
of favoritism, you would have thought the prize was a
highly sought-after front seat for a sold-out Broadway
mega-hit. To avoid bloodshed, names were put into a
hat in the office and the first five pulled had the thrill
of sitting on a cramped and uncomfortable school bus
crammed with screaming students to see a show that
catapulted no actor in it to stardom.

As part of the deal to see the play, the class had
to bring canned goods for the poor. They were also
to bring brown bag lunches to eat during the fifteen-
minute intermission, both as a break and to give them
energy to endure the almost endless second act. Some
of the boys carried in the boxes, which were separated
by content- the canned goods in some and the
lunches in others. They put them down where they
were instructed to along a wall in a hallway. Then we
sat down and attempted to comprehend the sad and
complicated play.

When the break came, I sent the same boys
to bring the boxes of lunches back so that their
classmates could wolf down their sandwiches and

snacks in the short time allowed. Soon they came running to me, empty handed and visibly upset.

"The boxes are gone!" cried Billy, a big blond boy who, up until now, had never raised his voice in front of me above a conversational tone. "Somebody stole our lunches!"

"Believe me, nobody here would want to steal your lunches. I'll go find them," I reassured them and raced off.

The layout of the school was like a labyrinth, with numerous wings and endless hallways that all seemed to lead to nowhere. I flew down the corridors with a pounding heart and finally found the office, where I quickly explained my dilemma to the sympathetic secretary. She told me kids from the senior class at the high school, who were in charge of taking the donated goods to an empty room, must have taken the box of lunches, as well. I wondered how they made it to their senior year and still couldn't tell the difference between a can of corn and a bagged sandwich.

By the time I found the room with the boxes of food and corralled some students to help me cart them back to the auditorium, the lights were dimmed and the play had resumed. If reading the kids' names on the bags in the dark was difficult, trying to pass them down the aisles quietly to their owners was next to impossible. We soon looked like the rudest theater audience in the world, with the students chewing on sandwiches and slurping down drinks. I moved my chair behind a pole and hid from the disapproving eyes of the teachers and chaperones from other schools.

While on the way back to the school, Ashley, having heard a strange word in the play, asked me what a lobotomy was. It was on the tip of my tongue to reply tartly, "A surgical procedure that was performed on members of the senior class at that school," but, instead, I answered in a polite, suitable, teacher-type way. "Something that talkative members of your class could use."

"Get to spend time with Jesus, hear his teachings, and spread the word of God," read the enticement on the "help wanted" poster I was hanging on the wall in the hallway. Beneath the words was a student's drawing of Jesus and a church. The headline read, "Disciples Wanted." It was a nicely done example for the project on religious advertisements I had given the students to show their creative skills, and hopefully score an easy good grade in the process. So far, posters on the wall lived up to my expectations, but the next one I put up brought the winning streak to a screeching halt.

"Become a disciple of Jesus," was written in crooked pink letters. The enticement beneath listed,"$5.00 an hour and a free Big Mac and fries." So, Jesus didn't even pay minimum wage or supply heart-healthy food! A dried fish and loaf of bread would have been better, and He seemed to have an abundant supply of those. Instead of a picture of a church or rendering of Jesus in a robe, there was a drawing of a five-dollar bill and something that resembled a squashed hamburger.

I was thinking a C- at the most as I taped up the awful ad when Marlene emerged from her classroom and, with a paper in hand and the usual hard look on her face, marched over to me.

"Durga forged her father's name on this test that was sent home to be signed," she said abruptly, shoving the paper in front of me and showing plainly that she held me personally responsible for permitting such a thing to happen, simply because Durga was in my homeroom.

"I'll talk to her about it," I said, taking the test in my hand and turning toward the wall to hang up the next ad, a signal that our verbal exchange had ended.

When I looked at the test a few moments later, I saw that the grade was a 78, and I wondered why Durga, a good student whose family was from a foreign country, would bother to forge a signature for a non-failing grade. I discovered the disturbing reason when I confronted a nervous Durga with the damming evidence at the end of classes that day.

"Durga, Mrs. Moore said that you forged your father's signature on this math test," I said in a non-threatening voice. "Is that true?"

Tears started from Durga's eyes and all she could do was stare at the ground and nod her head.

"But Durga, it wasn't even a failing grade. Why would you do that?"

Her streaming eyes met mine and there was a shamed look in her face when she blurted out, "Because he beats me if I get less than a B on a test."

The picture of this gentle, kindhearted girl being beaten was too much to be borne, and I struggled not to burst into tears myself.

"Durga, just go now," I told her, extremely embarrassed by my emotions and not wanting her to see me in a moment of weakness. She fled from the room, leaving me a few moments to collect my thoughts before having to go to the office and report this immediately to the principal, as was the proper procedure at that time.

I knew that Durga's family was from an Asian country with different customs. On the way to the office, I tried to justify to myself the fact that the type of punishment for failure that may be now unacceptable here was perfectly acceptable elsewhere. Plus, I remembered my own childhood friends from the Italian neighborhood being called *stupido* while receiving a simultaneous slap to the back of

the head for bringing home a bad report card. My
bad-boy spankings were also fondly recalled. And
even Proverbs proclaims, "The rod and rebuke
give wisdom." But it did no good. The image of the
shamefaced Durga was too overpowering.

Through the open door of the office I spotted Mrs.
Devilica seated at her desk, slowly and contentedly
chewing on a bitten-off hunk of a Hershey Bar like a
ruminating animal.

"May I come in? I have something that I have to
tell you," I asked politely, hoping for some help with
the sad, serious situation. The corner of her mouth
turned down and she waved me in, obviously put out
at the interruption of her snack time. I stood in front
of her desk and told the story of Durga while she
stared at me, an inscrutable expression on her face.
Finally, she spoke.

"Well, what are you going to do about it?"

"I just told you, that's what I'm going to do about
it," I answered, annoyed. "That's the procedure, isn't
it?"

"Don't get snippy with me!" she shot back, her
small elephant eyes becoming slits of rage and rapidly
disappearing into her fat face.

Somewhere in my brain, a slow fire rose, and
months of pent-up anger began to blot out everything
else. Then the rage broke, and I gave myself the

ultimate luxury of telling someone exactly what I thought of them.

"You know, it wouldn't kill you to not be so nasty to everyone all the time," I said savagely, feeling an intense momentary relieve at finally speaking my mind. "No wonder all your teachers quit on you last year."

"How dare you!" she screamed, quivering with insult. "Get out of my office!"

I turned on my heel and marched out, feeling euphoric but knowing I was doomed and could be let go any day. After enduring months of being treated like a thirteen-year-old, I was now behaving like one, but I was beyond the point of caring. My contract not being renewed that year was no big surprise.

I never discussed the situation of abuse for a bad grade again with Durga or Mrs. Devilica. In fact, from that point on, I rarely discussed anything with Mrs. Devilica. If she spotted me, she looked away and communicated by putting notes in my mailbox in the office. As for Durga, the few times her test grades dipped to the high seventies, I bumped them up to an 80 to avoid future bloodshed.

Besides Durga's sad case of physical abuse, I soon found myself embroiled in two problems of cruel bullying. I had no training concerning either and had to try to solve them both by instinct. One involved a boy's perceived sexual orientation, and the other a girl's pungent body odor, the latter being, I would suppose, much more easily correctable.

Diane, a nice girl in my homeroom, was still dealing with the recent death of her father. Her mother was beyond bizarre and was referred to by the office staff as Baby Jane because of her close resemblance to the Bette Davis character in the movie *What Ever Happened to Baby Jane?* who achieved her strange appearance by the sloppy application of mega amounts of face power, blond bleach, and mascara. The mother was a mess, but that wasn't Diane's fault. Her paternal grandparents, a kindly couple, paid her tuition since her dad's death, attempting to provide some stability in her life.

I first noticed the class's nonsensical cruelty toward Diane while taping a lobby card from the movie *The Sins of Jezebel* on the wall. I picked the card up at a flea market hoping that it might provide a nice contrast to the more conservative religious items – crosses, praying hands, nun dolls and the like– that decorated my classroom. Stepping back to admire the artwork, I saw that Johnny, who was passing out homework papers, was not handing them to Diane but, instead, leaning back and flinging them like Frisbees at her desk while his fellow classmates smirked or giggled. I glanced at Diane and saw the look of hurt and shame. Instantly, a tide of anger and grief for her humiliation swamped me, making my eyes sting. I couldn't reprimand the class now and embarrass Diane even more, but when the class left for recess I told Johnny to wait for a moment because I needed to have a word with him. Then I confronted him in the doorway.

"Why wouldn't you put the paper on Diane's desk?" I asked, looking him directly in the eye with an expression of reprove that implied no lies would be tolerated.

"What you did was very embarrassing to her."

"Because I didn't want to touch the desk or her," he replied, nervously but honestly. "She smells bad."

"What does she smell like?" I questioned, hoping it was some scent that could be easily changed, or at least masked over.

"Ferret pellets."

I had no idea what ferret pellets smelled like, but I could imagine it wasn't the most pleasant scent. And how could I mask the odor of the interior of an animal cage?

"Plus, she has cooties," Johnny childishly added.

"Cooties," I said, amused in spite of myself. I suddenly realized that my seventh graders, despite what they thought of their own maturity, were in many ways still kids. "I didn't think people even used that term anymore."

"Yeah, we still do," Johnny answered, sensing that my outrage was dissipating. "And she has them."

"No, she doesn't," I insisted. "And don't ever do that again. It was very cruel." It would have been wise to end the conversation there but, on an impulse, I decided to prove a point.

Without realizing that this gesture was in questionable taste, I pulled out my wallet, extracted a fifty- dollar bill, and held it up.

"I bet if I put this fifty-dollar bill on her desk you'd have no trouble picking it up," I said smugly, going to Diane's desk and laying the bill down in the dead center. Quick as a flash, Johnny raced to the desk, grabbed the bill, and then took off running past me into the hallway. I could still hear his laughter as he disappeared down the stairwell.

Realizing how ridiculous I would look chasing after him, and knowing that Johnny would have to return after lunch anyway, I started toward my desk to take up the task of correcting a sixth-grade test of the Ten Commandments. That's when I heard a girl call out my name. Turning, I saw a teary-eyed Diane walking toward me.

"Diane, you know you're not supposed to be up here during recess," I said, concerned about the impropriety of this situation following so closely on the heels of the fifty-dollar bill debacle.

"I'm sorry, Mr. Consorte, but I had to talk to you," she said between sobs.

"They say I smell and make fun of me. I don't smell, do I?"

"Of course not," I answered reassuringly, and honestly, since I had lost my sense of smell years before and, if she stunk to high heaven, I was mercifully spared.

"I'll take care of it, don't worry," I promised, not yet knowing how I would. "Here, take some Kleenex and go back to the cafeteria."

"Thank you, Mr. Consorte," she said between sniffles, and, tearing out some tissues from the box in my hand, she left for the lunchroom. As my eyes followed her slowly walking away, they were filled with a combination of pity for Diane and annoyance at being faced with yet another problem for which I didn't have a solution.

By now, a large part of the lunch break was over, leaving me little time to wolf down a tuna sandwich while wondering why one student had my fifty-dollar bill and another expected me to solve her stinky problem. And what did any of this have to do with teaching anyway?

The theory that fish is brain food must be true because, while taking the last bite of tuna, an idea flashed like a comet through my mind. I stopped by the office on my way to pick up the students in the cafeteria. Spotting some gossipy parents at the counter in front, I smiled automatically then had a whispered conference with Carol, who nodded her head in agreement with my plan.

"Johnny, hand it over," I said as the students passed through the doorway and into the classroom, thankful that, by some miracle, he was the last in line. The rest of the class, in the clamor and confusion of getting ready for the afternoon, wouldn't notice him handing me a fifty-dollar bill, which he did with a wide grin. With difficulty, I smothered a smile, as I wanted desperately to appear stern, but I realized the silly situation was my own fault for doing such a stupid thing to begin with.

"Diane, would you bring this test to the office and ask Mrs. Delancy to make thirty copies for me?" I asked politely after the students had settled down and the religion class on the Reformation started. Diane took the test and walked out the door, which I quickly closed behind her.

"Why did the church sell indulgences to people to forgive their sins?" asked Sandra, bewildered by the fact that a holy institution could do such a shameful thing.

"Because the church wanted the cash and people wanted an easy ticket to heaven," I answered quickly and honestly. "Anyway, we're switching to a quick lesson on 'do unto others as they would do unto you.' It's Matthew 7:12." I had quickly found the chapter and verse and wanted to impress the class with my knowledge of scripture.

"The way some of you are treating Diane is terrible, and I'm ashamed of you," I began sternly. "Here you are, praying one minute and being mean the next. And some of you being so cruel are altar servers. How hypocritical is that?" Those who had been singled out with a withering glare looked down at their desks, refusing to meet my eyes.

"I'll never understand what happiness a person gets by making someone else miserable," I said, now on a righteous roll. "Especially when the person being treated so badly has done nothing to deserve it."

Glancing around the room at the shamed students, I figured I had made my point and better finish up quickly. Carol couldn't delay Diane forever in the office by pretending the copying machine wasn't working properly and fiddling around with it.

"Those of you that did this, and you know who you are, certainly wouldn't enjoy having people call you names and do things to humiliate you. If I see any of this nonsense again, I'll call your parents and you can explain to them why you're being so nasty," I ended, and just in time, as the door opened and Diane entered with the copying and a nervous apology for taking so long.

"That's okay," I said, switching instantly from a scornful look aimed at the class to a benign smile directed toward her. "We were just discussing some of the teachings of Jesus. You didn't miss anything," I said quickly to cover my ruse before realizing that it didn't sound quite right.

But my words to the class weren't wasted. They stopped treating Diane like a leper, and, a few weeks later, Johnny told me that she didn't stink anymore. I assumed she somehow discovered the many benefits of a bar of soap and a daily bath.

Just as the Diane mess was cleaned up, another bullying incident began. Julian was an "at risk" boy from a bad neighborhood and he had a much rougher edge than the other students. He was also much older, being fourteen and in the sixth grade. Early in the year, I was made aware of a problem this age difference might produce.

It had been an ironclad rule since schoolboys no longer wore tunics that their shirts had to be tucked in. My teachers in elementary school threatened to tie pink ribbons to a boy's shirt when they spotted it untucked, which always led to a frenzied straightening up.

"We're letting Julian wear his shirt out because he might get excited looking at the girls," explained Mrs. Blackman in a very clinical tone.

It took a few seconds to understand the meaning of what she was telling me. Then, suddenly, I got the hang of it. I was glad he wasn't in my homeroom as I had no idea how to explain to other students, if asked, why Julian was being allowed to let his shirt flow freely why theirs had to be neatly tucked in.

Feeling sorry for Julian because of his disadvantaged background and almost total lack of academic skills, I did everything in my power to assist him in doing better. But as the year went by, the more unsavory aspects of his personality emerged and showed him to be a mean-spirited bully.

I had him seated in the front of the room for the dual purpose of keeping an eye on his behavior and getting as much work out of him as possible. He sat next to Carol's son, Michael, and one day, as Julian was settling into his seat, shirt hanging out as usual, I heard him call Michael a "little queer" and a "faggot." Michael looked down studiously at the book on his desk, already opened to the correct page, as always, and attempted to ignore him. I was incensed, but I tried to control my temper so as not make a scene and embarrass Michael by drawing the attention of the class to the situation.

"Julian, switch seats with Susan," I commanded. Seeing the hard expression on my face, he knew I meant business and, with just a tinge of attitude, he picked up his books and moved to Susan's desk, passing by her on route to her new seat beside a relieved and smiling Michael.

When passing by the office on my way out that evening, I spotted Carol standing behind the counter and, on an impulse, I stopped in and told her that Michael was being bullied and that I had taken care of it.

"It won't happen again, at least not in my presence," I assured her. Relieved, yet still concerned, she began to thank me profusely, but was interrupted by having to answer a ringing telephone. I waved goodbye and sped out, thinking the matter closed and not wanting to run into Mrs. Devilica.

That night, while I was enjoying the episode of *Seinfeld* in which Jerry and George are thought to be gay, the phone rang and I reluctantly answered it, annoyed at the poor timing.

"Hi Jimmy, I hope you don't mind me calling you at home?" It was Carol.

"Of course not," I lied, missing a punch line due to the interruption and hitting the record button on the remote to curtail the loss of more much-needed humor.

"Jimmy, I want to know what name Julian was calling Michael," Carol asked, a note of sadness in her voice. Then, before I could think of something better than the truth, she blurted out. "Was it faggot?"

Figuring there was no point in lying, I reluctantly told her that it was, sensing that I might be confirming her worst fears and wishing she would change the subject to any safer topic, like the weather or what she cooked for dinner.

"I thought so," she replied with a sigh of resignation in her voice. "This has happened before. He's such a good kid and he shouldn't have to go through this," Carol continued, and, though I couldn't have agreed more, I silently prayed for an end to this extremely uncomfortable conversation. Instead, it quickly got worse.

"Do you think Michael's gay?" she asked, placing me in the unenviable position of having to pass judgment on the sexual orientation of her son. But all behavioral arrows pointed in that direction. His mannerisms were far from manly and all his friends were girls. Then there was the incident that occurred during one of the chess matches that I had organized.

While shopping in a toy store, I found a few plastic chess sets with the reduced price of a dollar each, so I bought them and taught the students how to play the game during indoor recesses. As an added treat, I brought in my own beautiful set that was based on the Revolutionary War, the pieces being historic characters and soldiers. Of course, the kids all wanted to play with that set. During one rainy recess, Michael and one of the more outspoken girls were in the middle of a match, moving around the red and blue figures, when the girl called me over to their desk.

"Michael keeps making the king kiss the soldiers and I'm going to be sick!" she loudly complained, staring up at me while clutching her stomach for dramatic effect.

Thinking quickly, I recovered the situation by replying, "Michael sure knows his history. He's just demonstrating the way men expressed affection in those days. In fact, the French men kissed each other on each cheek, right Michael?"

Michael nodded and smiled up at me and the girl was mollified, but the event left little doubt in my mind as to the coming-of fantasies that were forming in Michael.

Although I was quite sure of my suspicions, there was no way I intended to be the one to break such news to his mother. So I answered Carol's pointed question with an officious lie, figuring one more venial sin on my soul shouldn't be enough to send me to Satan.

"I don't think so," I said slowly, pretending to give the subject extended and careful consideration. "He's just a very caring and sensitive kid, and you should be proud of him," I continued, hoping the soothing words would settle the matter.

"Thank you for saying that," she said sincerely, breathing an audible sigh of relief. "I have to run and pick up Michael at his acting class. I'll see you tomorrow at school."

"Goodbye. See you tomorrow," I finished, just
in time to hear Seinfeld end the sitcom saying, "I'm
not gay. Not that there's anything wrong with that."
Ironically, that line, designed by writers of a comedy
for a laugh, seemed to sum up my conversation with
Carol, and it left me with hope that Michael's situation
would have a happy ending. Then I picked up a pile of
papers to correct and, with a silent curse, took off five
points from the top one on the pile for no name.

In April, the pope decided to pay a visit to the
New York area. Almost as amazing was that I, of all
people, was elected to take the altar servers from the
school to see him. Actually, the job landed in my lap
by default, as no one else at the school wanted to give
up a Saturday to do it, not even the resident nun.
I had never seen a pope before, and here was one
almost at my doorstep. The choice between the time
and economics of traveling thousands of miles to the
Vatican to view one or twenty minutes down the road
for the same sight was a no brainer.

The catch came that Saturday morning when the
altar servers were waiting in front of the church for
the bus that we were sharing with kids from other
Catholic schools in the area. Father Benzitti handed
me a long list of names and informed me that I would
be responsible for everyone on the bus. The only
other "adults" for supervision that holy day were some
female fifteen-year-old religious instructors who

would prove to be less than worthless when it came to maintaining even a minimum amount of discipline.

At least we lucked out with the weather, as April in New York runs the gamut of pleasant warmth with budding daffodils to a climate that is polar bear friendly. It was a long day of watching thousands of Catholic school kids milling about and smiling seminarians dancing in circles. The lines for the few food concessions were hours long, so waiting in them took up the entire morning. Finally, about four in the afternoon, the pope arrived in his popemobile and the show started. If nothing else, after two thousand years of practice, Catholics can put on a good show when called on to do so. It was beautiful, especially the part with the sun setting and "Ave Marie" being sung.

Then, suddenly, it ended, and the now tired twenty thousand attendees headed en masse for the single nine-foot wide fence opening. When we finally found our bus among the hundreds of others, we piled in and the useless supervisors headed for the back seats and instantly went to sleep. After an interminable delay getting out of the lot, the bus headed back toward the school and the students from the other schools started smacking one another. Obviously, viewing the pope and hearing his message of peace left no impression on them, and I was forced to spend the trip pacing up and down the bus breaking up fights, which would only erupt again as soon as my back was turned.

What interested me most about Pope Benedict was the fact that he had been a member of the Hitler Youth. My father had served in Europe during World War II, and his stories about the brainwashing and fanaticism of the German children fascinated me as a child. Only boys, they fought to the death during the twilight of the Third Reich, and he was forced to shoot many of them. The only other person I had met that was in the Hitler Youth was Kurt, a dishwasher in my father's restaurant. When I worked with him one New Year's Eve, he drank the remains of customers' drinks in the dirty glasses and, at ten o'clock, passed out cold on the floor, leaving me alone to wash five hundred customers' dishes, glasses, and silverware. So, of the two people I saw from the Hitler Youth, one was a drunken bum and the other a pope.

The month of May arrived, ushering in a whirlwind of religious activities. First Communion, Confirmation, and a somewhat strange ceremony called The Crowning of Mary. I managed to evade the Communion, but I had no choice, being the religion teacher, but to attend the Confirmation for the eighth-grade class. Sad to say, some of them were more deserving of the wrath of God than His benevolence. Mrs. Blackman had decorated the corkboard outside her classroom with pictures of the eighth graders with flames representing the Holy Spirit settling on their heads. I was tempted to perversely place the flames beneath their pictures portraying them as roasting heretics, figuring that some of the sixth-grade boys would probably be blamed for the dastardly deed. But I let go of the fantasy, realizing it was as far from professional behavior as was possible. And I might get caught.

However, I did get some satisfaction during Confirmation class by telling them, with a concealed grin, that part of the Confirmation process, as I remembered it from decades ago, involved the bishop asking difficult questions in front everyone in the packed pews, and then slapping the students' faces to confirm them. The expressions of panic and concern on the eighth graders' faces were priceless and served as some payback for the inattention and smirks I had received from them since September. At the Confirmation, it was almost amusing to observe the incorrigibly bad students behaving in church like little angels for the benefit of the captive audience of adoring parents and relatives. Lions transformed into lambs for the solemn ceremony.

Sitting through the service and then making a dash for the church door was my plan, but it was foiled a few weeks before the event when an aggressive Japanese mother of one of the eighth graders spotted me outside the office and dive bombed me like a kamikaze.

"Mr. Consorte, you come P.J.'s Confirmation party, okay, okay," she shot out as I was backed against the wall. "P.J. like you and he want you there, so you be there." It wasn't stated as a question, but rather a command.

"When is it?" I asked, hoping for a major conflict of obligations.

"Right after Confirmation ceremony. Here invitation. See you there," she said with finality, producing an envelope from her pocketbook and flinging it at my hand.

"Thank you," I said with a sardonic smile, the expression being lost on her as she had already managed a ninety-degree turn on a red high heel and took off out the front door.

P.J. was one of my best students and had given me few problems, probably out of sheer terror that any incident would be reported to his tiger of a mother. So, after snooping around via Carol and finding out that none of the nasty teachers from the school were going, I decided to appear at his party.

Upon entering the catering hall where P.J.'s celebration was being held, I expected to be directed to a small private room set up for maybe fifty guests, at most. After all, my own Confirmation decades before had consisted of a dinner out with my immediate family and a few religious cards from some aunts. But when I walked into the room pointed out to me by the *maître d'*, my surprised eyes took in what looked like a good-sized wedding in full swing.

Spread out at tables around a large dance floor were at least two hundred people. All were afforded an unobstructed view to feast adoring eyes on an elevated table where P.J. was perched at the center, enthroned like royalty. In front of the boy king, a streaming video showing a litany of his achievements ran continuously. No attempt at feigned modesty here.

Before I could get to a chair and hide out for the afternoon, his mother spied me and sped over.

"Welcome, Mr. Consorte, so nice of you to come. You make speech about P.J., okay," she commanded, sinking shiny, neon red fingernails into my arm and dragging me to the middle of the dance floor.

"Quiet, everyone, I have announcement to make," she screamed, silencing the submissive audience instantly. "This Mr. Consorte, P.J.'s teacher, and he so happy to have P.J. as student that he want to give speech about him."

Caught totally off guard and embarrassed at suddenly being the center of attention, I silently cursed her while speaking in respectful tones about P.J., saying something about what an honor it was to have been his teacher and how happy I was to be able to share this day with him and his family. When the clapping began, I saw some congenial teaching colleagues at a table with an empty chair and quickly made my way to them.

With the horror of having to make an impromptu speech over, I attempted to enjoy the dinner, making headway with what looked something like duck when a silly floorshow began.

P.J., who had vacated his throne and vanished a few moments before, dramatically reappeared on the dance floor dressed in a kung fu outfit. To the sounds of stirring music provided by the DJ, and cheered on by his captive audience, he performed a series of karate chops and kicks. I politely applauded along with the rest, waiting to see if he would chop a piece of wood in two for a finale. If no wood could be obtained, I reasoned that his mother's neck would make a wonderful substitute.

After suffering the endless afternoon of P.J.'s party, the Crowning of Mary celebration a few days later was short and simple: a girl in a white dress (big surprise) climbs a ladder to put a crown of flowers on the statue of Mary's head. After seating my students in the church pews, all I had to do was make sure that they sang the required song and then shut up when the priest made his speech.

"Oh Mary, we crown you with blossoms today, queen of the flowers, queen of the May," they sang, while a girl in the third grade carefully climbed up

the wobbly ladder and placed the crown lopsided on Mary's head.

In the middle of this sweet ceremony, Sandy, who was seated directly ahead, turned a sick face to me and said that she didn't feel well. Before I could even get up, she puked in the pew.

Commotion ensued as the students near Sandy, holding their noses and saying "ewwww", scrambled to get as far from the puke as possible. Sandy, mortified, her uniform covered with her recently downed lunch of scarcely-digested chicken nuggets and corn chips, fled in tears down the aisle toward the church entrance as all the students turned to see what I'm sure they considered a much better show than the pious one that just preceded it.

At least Mrs. Devilica couldn't blame me for this mishap, knowing I have no control over the internal miseries of my students.

But, back in the classroom, I told the class that, in the future, if anyone felt sick, don't bother to ask permission, just run for the bathroom, or at least the nearest garbage can. In other words, anywhere away from me!

It was finally time for the eighth-grade graduation. A week after that glorious, longed-for event would be the party in the classroom on the last day of school.

I had told the students the week before that I wouldn't be returning. It wasn't an easy undertaking as, when I saw the effect of my words in their startled eyes, full realization came to me of what was soon to happen. I would no longer be their teacher, and I would probably never see them again. Most of them I would miss acutely. It was too early in my teaching career to realize that this strange feeling of loss would occur in some form, depending, of course, on your fondness for a class, almost every June.

Most of the parents were upset and wanted to make up a petition to keep me there. I was touched but told them please don't. It would only cause more problems and, even if they somehow convinced that old harridan to keep me on, she would continuously come up with innovative ways to harass me. So, thanks but no thanks.

But Johnny's mother decided to enact her own form of revenge. She had been a wide-eyed witness to the shenanigans that went on at that dance in October, and now, in a fit of righteous anger, she dialed-up some officials in the archdiocese and spilled the beans on certain chaperones' bad behavior.

So began an investigation into the events that occurred that evening, with rumors and lies flying behind closed classroom doors and fear consuming the office. Those involved, Marge, Marlene, and Carol, were near having nervous breakdowns, but I couldn't muster a spark of sympathy for them, as they had been the authors of their own miseries. It was interesting to watch, as a detached observer, their mad scramble to cast the blame on each other to save their own guilty hides. "Let those without sin cast the first stone" was a teaching tossed aside. Yet, despite the dread that the four horsemen were galloping down the halls past the taped-up students' artwork of spring flowers, plans somehow went forward for the final exams, parties, and graduation.

It would have been simple for me to have made Mrs. Devilica's difficult situation even worse by just calling out sick for those last two weeks and having someone else deal with my year-end duties. Thoughts of this were tantalizing, but I remembered the true Catholic school story of the nun on her deathbed and the principal still bringing the report cards to the hospital for the dedicated nun to fulfill her final duty before receiving her heavenly reward. So, I decided that a good scare would suffice.

The graduation would, of course, take place in the church. The teachers were to walk behind the students from the school hall to the church and sit in a special row behind them. The proceedings were to begin at 10 A.M. on a Saturday morning. We were supposed to be mustered in the hall and ready to march a half hour earlier.

The morning of the graduation, I arrived at the school on time, parked two blocks away so as to be undetected, and hid out, passing the time reading an article in *Psychology Today* on narcissism.

When the church bells started ringing, I knew it was ten and the procession was about to begin. I quickly walked the two blocks, saw the line of students and teachers making their way to the church, and slipped into my assigned position. Mrs. Devilica, panting from the effort of propelling her body forward in the heat, saw me and drew a visible sigh of relief.

The ceremony was beautiful as the church was decorated with big white bows and flowers. The students rose to the occasion and acted demure and sweet, making me suddenly wonder why they could not always be this way. As for two of the teachers and the principal, whatever was going on in their minds didn't show on their faces, as they hid their emotions behind professional facades. That is, until it was time for communion.

Mrs. Devilica, being a deacon, was allowed to hand out the hosts when an extra hand was needed. As the church was packed and there were a lot of takers that day, she waddled up to the altar. "Please don't put her on our side of the altar," I prayed fervently, and in vain, as she picked up her ration of hosts and parked her wide load at the railing directly in front of my pew, looming more like the personification of the deadly sin of gluttony than

a ministering angel of God. When it was time for
the teacher row to get up and go to the altar, they
duly filed out without me. The thought of taking
communion from her was abhorrent, as I would more
likely be tossed into the third circle of hell than be
forgiven of sins. So I knelt alone in the pew, staring
at her with a studied nonchalance as she glared at me
while handing out the hosts.

Finally, the last day of school arrived. The
festivities involved a party in the classroom from eight
to nine-thirty, followed by the students wiping down
the desks, then dragging them into the hallway and
stacking them on top of one another. Then the report
cards were handed out and were received with delight
or dread.

The theme of the party was the beach, so I
decorated the classroom with Annette Funicello
beach movie posters and played Beach Boys music.
I had even purchased an animated Hawaiian
hula-dancing doll that shook her hips to a fast tune.
Expecting to finish the year with as little ceremony as
possible, I was emotionally unprepared for what was
about to occur.

Sitting at my desk, filling out report cards fifteen
minutes before going to the yard to lead the students
in for the last time, the classroom was suddenly
flooded with parents bearing affectionate goodbyes
and gifts. That was tough to take, but when I got to

the yard and saw my students with their arms full of presents and cards, it took an almost superhuman effort on my part not to break down and make a total fool of myself in front of them. It would have been an easier ending for me to deal with if the kids had bought me nothing and told me to drop dead!

The floor at the front of my classroom was lined with gifts, not only from my homeroom but from the sixth-grade students, as well. One boy even made me a large diorama of a cardboard Fort Sumter mounted on a two-foot platform of wood. I also received a huge handmade card from the seventh-grade class with a wise owl on the front and the students' names and goodbyes inside. Most touching of all was a simple card that a boy, Anthony, hand delivered to me while thanking me for being his teacher that year. In it, he sincerely apologized for his bad behavior and was sorry if it caused me any trouble. It was one of the very few times in my teaching career that I was to receive a heartfelt apology that wasn't forced from a student by a fearsome principal. I still have the letter, saved all these years as a reminder that middle school students are actually capable of feeling remorse.

As the kids gobbled up the goodies provided by the parents and played games, I wondered how I would ever cram all this stuff in my little Mustang convertible. And it would take forever to carry it down the stairs and to the car. Then I saw students from the other homerooms carrying their teachers' presents to their cars and decided to do the same. I asked Johnny and Danny to bring my gifts to the car.

They left the room with their hands full. A moment later they returned carrying the same bags and with aggravated expressions on their faces.

"Mrs. Devilica said we couldn't carry the presents for you. We're sorry," Danny apologized, putting down the bags.

"That's okay, thanks anyway," I responded, realizing that, of course, she would put a roadblock in the path of anything that would make my life easier, even in my last hours at the school.

At nine-thirty, the desks were wiped down with Windex and happily pushed out into the hallway and piled on top of one another against the walls. It was now time to give out the report cards. On an impulse, I decided to have the hula-dancing doll do it. Her arms were stretched out in front of her and I placed the first report card on top of them to give the illusion that she was a swaying giver. Then I put on Connie Francis singing "Vacation," the kids lined up, and we were set to go.

One of the first report cards was Danny's, which he took and, for some reason, started laughing as I looked down to find the next card. Every student after Danny giggled as they got their card. Some laughed hysterically, and I congratulated myself on the great idea of having the dancing doll distribute them.

When the last card was given out and the students were comparing grades, I walked around to the front of my desk and was suddenly shocked to see that someone had pulled down the doll's top piece and pushed back her lei, exposing her humongous plastic breasts. So, this was the mystery of the merriment - report cards presented by a dancing doll with a big, exposed bosom! I quickly pulled up her top and hit the off switch. For a moment I was mortified, and then I smirked, picturing in my mind the reaction of Mrs. Devilica if found out and realizing that this was the perfect ending for such a messed-up year.

I wanted to just skulk out of the school, but the seemingly dozens of trips bringing all the gifts to the car unfortunately took me past the prying eyes in the office. On the next-to-last trip, Mrs. Devilica nailed me.

"Mr. Consorte, may I see you for a moment?" she murmured, her deceptively sweet tone instantly putting me on high alert. I followed her for the last time into her office and sat across from her, separated by a desk and a year of conflicting bad memories.

"As you probably know, the school has had inquiries from the archdiocese regarding the behavior of some of the staff at the dance back in October. Whoever went to the archdiocese told them that you had nothing to do with the situation that occurred. Obviously, the good reputation of the school is in jeopardy. Can you tell me anything you know about this?" she cooed, forcing a smile that died before it reached the full expanse of her face.

"You big hypocrite," I thought. "Now you're being nice because I have information you desperately need to save your big ass." My first impulse was to get up and walk out. It's not as if I hadn't done that before. Then I thought, "Why not tell her everything and let her see just how sleazy some of her favorite faculty members are?" Shakespeare surely knew human nature when he wrote "revenge is a dish best served cold."

So, without mentioning Carol, I gleefully spilled the beans on the other two culprits without feeling a tinge of remorse. Mrs. Devilica, her face devoid of any emotion, took it all in.

"God as my witness, that's exactly what happened," I concluded with a flourish. "Now I'll leave you with what remains of your conscience. Goodbye." And to give more weight to my words, I stood up and left the room, pleased with my dramatic exit.

Somehow, I crammed all the gifts into the car and was about to slide into the driver's seat when Marge suddenly appeared beside me.

"Well, Jimmy, I'm sorry things didn't work out this year," she said with an attempt at sincerity. Maybe she was sorry, but who cared now?

"Come on, let's go have a cigarette together and talk before you leave," she suggested with a sly smile while glancing around the schoolyard for the most concealing shrubbery. "We can hide behind those rhododendron bushes."

"Sure, why not?" I responded, reaching into the console of my car for a pack of cigarettes, the absurdity of the situation appealing to an immature sense of escapade.

We pushed our way through the branches, seated ourselves with our backs leaning against the school, and lit up like we were both fourteen years old. Then she started pumping me for information, which I sensed all along was the purpose behind this sudden camaraderie. My replies verged on riddles, much to her chagrin. After two cigarettes, she threw in the towel and suggest we go before we got caught. We both stood up, Marge groaning with the effort, brushed the mulch off our damp behinds, and, looking to see that the coast was clear, slipped back out of the hedges and into the sunlight.

"What will you do now?" were her final words to me as I opened the door to my car.

"Oh, I'll get by," I replied, not daring to tell her that another teaching job was waiting in the wings.

"Maybe I'll write a story about my year here entitled *What Not to Do as a New Teacher,*" I joked. She didn't laugh, and I drove my Mustang out of the parking lot for the last time. Glancing into the side view mirror, I spotted Marge re-entering the portals of the school, beyond which pain is practiced. I imagined that a severe grilling with Mrs. Devilica holding Marge's feet to the fire was in store, but her squared shoulders and head held high led me to surmise that she had already concocted some devious but credible lies as her first line of defense.

As I drove down the street I wondered irrelevantly if the inquisition of Marge and Marlene would begin with a prayer, as it seemed everything in the school did. In this case, they would surely need one.

Chapter 11

Grace in the Ghetto

A week went by before I called Mr. Thomas as I didn't want to bother him until the hectic days of wrapping up a school year subsided. He told me that he was almost completely sure of the opening for me, as he had heard from reliable sources that the teacher who was leaving had already moved to New Jersey and signed a contract at a school there, even though she had signed a contract at his school for the next year.

"But why would she do that?" I asked.

"She hates me and is just doing it to be spiteful. She's thinking that when she finally tells me that she won't be back, I'll have to rush to get a teacher with only a few weeks to go before school starts."

"God, that's terrible," I exclaimed, realizing now that disagreements in schools weren't isolated to Our Lady of the Holy Rosary Beads and wondering if any school was free from turmoil.

"But don't worry, you have the job, and as soon as I hear from her I'll call you to come in and sign a contract," Mr. Thomas reassured me.

Just as he predicted, the purposely delayed call came from New Jersey two weeks before the start of the new school year. As soon as Mr. Thomas hung up with her, he called me.

"Can you come in this afternoon?" he asked. "You can sign the contract and I'll show you the school."

An hour later, I was seated before him signing my name on a paper stating my next year's salary and my promise to promote Catholic values.

"I'm so happy to have you here," smiled Mr. Thomas. "You have no idea what we went through last year."

"Hummmph!" I thought. Whatever it was would pale into insignificance compared to the nonsense at Our Lady of The Holy Rosary Beads.

"The young guy I hired gave Sister Veronica, his fellow teacher, the finger behind her back right in front of his class after she reprimanded him."

"You're kidding!" I said, thinking that this was a step down from even the low standards I had already witnessed.

"I wish I were. One of the students told me and I had to let the teacher go."

"Was his name, by any chance, John Parker?" I asked, thinking of the young guy that sat at my table during the teacher orientation and acted so obnoxiously. It seemed like something he'd do.

"Yes, that's him," he said surprised. "How would you know him?"

"We sat at the same table during the teacher orientation. He didn't behave very well there. In fact, Mr. Masala got pretty aggravated with him."

"I'm not surprised. He was replaced with Sister Agatha. What a mistake that was," Mr. Thomas said, shaking his head with regret. "She was in her late seventies and I could see she was beginning to lose it, but I didn't realize how far gone she was until a parent came to me and said her son's class had gotten the same homework assignment from Agatha for the last two months. She finally had to be dragged out of the classroom in a straitjacket right in front of the students."

I just stared at him, thinking that those two classroom follies would be tough, if not impossible, acts to follow.

"Let me show you around the school. And you can call me Greg, except in front of the kids," he said in a joking tone while smiling and rising from his seat. What a pleasure it was to be shown kindness by a boss after the brutal treatment dished out to me daily by that last beast. But during the first few moments of the tour, my smile became more and more forced.

The floors of the long hallways were filthy, the walls marked-up, and, above, lights were burned out in the fixtures. But as bad as the dim and dingy corridors were, my classroom, if possible, was worse.

The crud-encrusted blinds were broken and hanging at crazy angles, a closet door was held together with duct tape, and the desks and chairs were defaced with answers to tests probably taken decades ago. A passing glance into the boys' room as we strolled by made me want to go home and throw up! I figured it would take a hardworking cleaning crew two weeks of back-breaking labor to bring the place to the point where the Board of Health could be kept at bay. I had never seen a dirty school before, so it was an understandable shock to view such a vista of sad neglect.

Yet Mr. Thomas seemed not to notice the mess surrounding him, and he conducted this tour of assorted horrors as majestically as if he were presenting the Palace of Versailles.

We exited the school through a translucent glass door that screamed for a scouring with Windex and walked across a front yard that was spewed with litter toward an ancient brick building that housed the cafeteria and gym. Built over a century before, it had served first as a church and then a school. It was interesting to think of all the students who had studied and worshiped there, celebrating countless religious holidays and graduations. I would later learn of the school's illustrious history, but its glory days were long past, and now, with some windows boarded over with plywood and a façade of missing bricks, it looked like a prime candidate for a demolition ball.

As bad as it appeared on the outside, the inside was worse. Peeling paint, dusty and faded curtains on the stage, and garbage on the dirty floor told only part of the story, but it was enough. Having spent years working in sales, where a huge premium was placed on appearances and first impressions, my initial thought was, "Why would any parent spend money to send their kids to this place?"

The next couple of days were spent desperately trying to make my classroom fit for human habitation. With all the intense physical labor and late summer heat, I actually sweated off a few pounds. The place was slowly transformed. Though far from sparkling, at least the room was neat and clean.

Three days before the start of school, I realized the less than useless custodian had no intention of cleaning the glass doors, bathrooms, or teachers' lounge. All he did in the two weeks before school started was wax the hallway floors without cleaning them first and replace the burned-out bulbs in hallways which, now brightly lit, looked even worse than before.

Surprisingly, no one at the school seemed bothered by any of this. So, I cleaned as much of the building as I could, even the beyond disgusting bathrooms, where bottles of bleach were consumed before I could tell the true color of the floors. The old proverb about it being better to light a candle (or clean a bathroom) than curse the darkness was proven correct once again. It was easier to just clean the place than get disgusted viewing this depressing monument to neglect every day.

The teachers at St. Dymphna's were your usual assortment of personality types, spanning the spectrum of nice and efficient to half out of their minds. But, after the debacle at the last school, I was seriously determined to get along well with all. That road, at times, would prove rocky, but, for now, it was smoothed with pleasant smiles.

Some supervisory tasks were easier at St. Dymphna's, and some more difficult and dangerous. The teachers here spent a lot more time with the morning, bus, yard, and cafeteria duties, the last two in a tie for the title of "most likely to make you wish you were dead." Having yard duty meant escorting one hundred students in a line across the parking lot and to a public park that might be populated during the course of the day by drug addicts, hookers, gang members, and the homeless. Name the fringe group that you were trying to keep your students from ever joining and there they were, in all their grungy glory.

But not to fear. To control the students and keep undesirables at bay, I was well armed with an anachronistic big bell and whatever shreds of authority it might still command.

As an additional bonus, before the students were allowed to enter the park, I had to proceed first with a broom and dust pan to scout out and sweep up any hypodermic needles and used condoms that may have been carelessly tossed aside after the thrill of using them was through.

The cafeteria, though certainly less dangerous, had its own collection of horrors to bedevil whoever was in charge. Cram a hundred energetic, screaming kids into a basement with a low ceiling and the sound soon approaches a sonic boom. Once again, the big hand bell and a stern expression was the sole means of control. On one memorable occasion, when the students were totally unruly, getting out of their seats and tossing string beans at one another (they never threw a chicken nugget or piece of pizza, as those prized food sources were always gleefully devoured), I rang the bell so forcefully the clapper came off and flew across the room. Fortunately, no one was hit in the head or I would have become the subject of a lawsuit and a bizarre bad teacher story in the papers.

On the unfortunate days that you had yard or cafeteria duty, you were left with a whole fifteen minutes to wolf down your lunch. If you had to use the bathroom, your dining time was cut to what you could quickly cram in your mouth. Some days, I had a sandwich with two bites taken out of it sitting in my desk drawer until the students departed at the end of the day, when I could finally finish the now half-stale meal.

But these inconveniences were more than balanced by the supportive principal and the two teachers whose classrooms were closest to mine. One was a stern but kind older nun, the other a funny and happy gay man of Asian descent. As Sister's classroom was between ours, she referred to her situation jokingly as "the rose between the thorns." She wore a full habit "for effect," she explained. The students always instantly obeyed her requests, a record I never came close to matching. When I asked how she did it, she gave me a classic nun reproving look and said, "My face." If that's what it took to command respect, I would gladly have donned a habit myself.

Mr. Chin had his own method of control. Having been raised strictly by a "tiger mom" (as a child, if he dared bring home a bad grade, she forced him to kneel bare-kneed on a piece of spiky fruit while she smiled and pushed down on his shoulders), and then doing a two-year stint in the strongly disciplined

Asian army, he came more than prepared to tolerate no nonsense. Gentle by nature, he could not have been kinder to the kids. But if they dared not do his bidding, he reverted to his background training and, with ruler in hand and menacing dark eyes riveted on them, sternly barked out orders, reminding me of the prison camp commander in the movie *The Bridge on the River Kwai*.

The first day of school found the students assembled in the front yard. A glance out the window clued me in that the makeup of the student body here was somewhat different than that of my former school as it consisted entirely of minorities, mostly Hispanic. The first student from my homeroom to enter and say hello was a nice boy named Jose. Six years later, in a sad irony, his younger brother would be the last student I would see exit the school forever.

Before the first day ended, I decided that something had to be done to stop the endless distractions from the bleak, crime-ridden city just outside the classroom windows. Aside from ear splitting sounds produced by passing police cars, ambulances, and fire trucks, the simple solution of lowering the blinds all the way down, combined with the constantly changing, engaging decorations in the classroom, managed to visually close out the rest of the world.

But I couldn't easily erase the disruptive home life of many of the students. At least half of the record cards for my homeroom had a big blank space where the name of a father belonged. Most of the others displayed names and addresses different from the mothers. Some of the students had the same mother but different last names. On occasion, mothers would come to the school with their new boyfriends, who appeared about two years older than their eighth grade sons. These men were referred to by the students as their "uncle," which was a cute euphemism for "Mom's new boyfriend."

All these loose family affiliations turned parent-teacher nights into an interesting guessing game. There were some relationships the teachers could never figure out, as with each new school year mothers would show up with different men and children, usually "cousins" of other students. For someone who had been raised in the era of TV shows like *Father Knows Best* and *The Donna Reed Show*, this was a horror and hard to relate to. It was small wonder that a considerable number of the students hated to go home at the close of the school day. But you work with what you have, and, despite the somewhat sad circumstances, most of the kids were pretty good.

After only a month into the new school year, there was a principals' conference where Mr. Thomas had the distinct misfortune of being seated at the same table with Mrs. Devilica, who had discovered that he had hired me without first checking with her, conveniently circumventing the proper protocol. Seriously chagrined, she attacked him as soon as he sat down.

"I just wanted to let you know that she's trying to make trouble for you," Mr. Thomas told me after summoning me to his office the following morning. "I had heard from others that she's very vindictive, and now I believe it. She's probably going to report me to Mr. Masala, who got me this principal's job, and I'm sure to catch hell from him," he said sadly, then smiled automatically as some passing students greeted him.

My drive home from work that day was filled with worry that Mr. Thomas might get in trouble for helping me out. I didn't work for Mrs. Devilica anymore, so why should she care where I was or what I did? She was a lethal combination of being both vicious and relentless, and apprehension over what trouble she could cause meant no rest on my pillow that night.

Deliverance came in a form least expected when I turned on the TV news the next morning and stared in shocked amazement at the newscaster announcing,"Mr. Masala, supervisor of Catholic school teachers, has been arrested on charges of child molestation. We'll be right back with this and other stories right after this commercial break." I sank down on the couch and impatiently waited out what seemed the longest commercial break in the history of television, silently vowing never to buy any of the products being touted.

"Mr. Masala was arrested today on charges of child molestation. The acts took place a decade ago when he was principal of St. Thomas School. Three men in their twenties have come forward with these accusations, claiming the molestation occurred when they were in the sixth grade at St. Thomas. This clip shows Mr. Masala at the Italian Festa last year."

The video showed Mr. Masala, a gleam of delight in his eyes, shoving a cannoli into his big, blubbery mouth while the sound system in the background belted out the Rosemary Clooney tune "Botch-A-Me." I figured that the person in the news crew that put this segment together had a strange sense of humor.

What a startling and almost supernatural coincidence that Mr. Masala should be tossed into jail just at the right moment. Was the guardian angel I shared my seat with in Sister Catherine's catechism class so long ago still hanging around and looking out for me? Now I was glad I made room for her. My bedtime companion that night turned out not to be anxiety after all, but deep wonder.

As soon as I saw Mr. Thomas enter his office the next morning, I raced in behind him and asked if he had heard the news.

"I couldn't believe it," he replied.

"Maybe it's not true," I said, providing Mr. Masala with the benefit of the doubt. "Sometimes people make up these stories just to get money."

"I made some calls after I saw the news and was told by those in the know that he had been thoroughly investigated, and it seems that the allegations have merit."

"Do you know what he did?" I asked, burning with curiosity.

"For one, when he was principal of St. Thomas School, he would take sixth-grade boys for driving lessons in a nearby cemetery. They had to sit on his lap when they drove the car. That's one of the ways he got his jollies. Need I go on?" he said, raising an eyebrow.

"No, I get the general idea. That is gross!" I exclaimed in the correct tone of moral righteousness, although the image in my mind of the car nonsense was so bizarre as to be almost, but not quite, comical. And didn't Mr. Masala wonder that at some point in their lives the boys would find out that a car couldn't have both a stick shift and an automatic?

"I'm glad you think so,"
Mr. Thomas replied.

Before we could continue our conversation, the teacher who had the morning duty in front of the school burst into the office, visibly upset, holding the hand of a screaming little boy who appeared to have something small and gray in the middle of his forehead. She breathlessly explained the situation in one quick, continuous sentence. "David was running around outside and fell and hit his head on the pavement and a piece of gravel got lodged in his forehead and I can't pick it out and he has to be taken to the hospital and have his parents called."

Sensing that this was the end of the discussion on the sins and transgressions of Mr. Masala, and, getting nauseous looking at the poor, crying little boy with a rock in his forehead, I ducked out of the office.

So, we never heard of Mr. Masala again. He became relegated to one of the topics of conversation better left untouched. We never heard from Mrs. Devilica, either. She probably got caught up in the many everyday problems of running a school and decided that they were more important than an occurrence from the past. On occasion, I would spot her at the food table during the teacher conferences and discreetly kept my distance as I didn't need a bagel that desperately. Finally, I was able to push the thought of her into the trash room of my mind and shut the door upon it.

Although my time teaching at St. Dymphna's was mostly enjoyable, especially compared to the hellish atmosphere at my previous school, it was not without its problems. The fact that it was located in a ghetto was one, but I quickly learned to deal with the danger by running from the parking lot to the school, key in hand, on dark winter mornings, ignoring the occasional gunshots from robberies in the string of stores on the next street over, and pretending that the bullet holes in the brickwork on one side of the school were merely a mirage.

Other problems were caused by the fact that some of the teachers, and the monsignor, were relics from a bygone era that was fading fast. Father Sullivan was in his seventies, and, instead of being the kindly, happy-go-lucky Irish priest presented in Hollywood films, he was about as friendly as Lucifer. An avid basketball fan, he once told the kids assembled at Mass that he would break all their legs if the Knicks lost the next game. Another of his light-hearted statements to the students was that if he ever found out that they were misbehaving in public while dressed in the school uniform, he'd kill them. Never once did he come into the school to talk to the students, not even to wish them a merry Christmas. Mr. Congeniality he was not.

Also, his sermons could hardly be called uplifting. He must have been allergic to the hosts, because every time they were unveiled he had a coughing fit all over them, turning communion into a health-risking affair. After the Mass he was supposed to talk to the students about the faith, but that consisted of badgering them with tough Bible questions, which would continue until someone knew the answer. I would secretly whisper the answer to a student seated near me to put an end to the torture.

Yet when Father Sullivan needed the students to fill the church for show, he would call for a command performance. His mother's funeral called for the entire school, including the kindergarten kids, who had no real conception of death, to attend. The funeral was routine, yet seemingly endless (coffin wheeled in to the sound of "Amazing Grace," Mass, eulogy, ad nauseam). The younger students fidgeted while the older ones looked bored to desperation. Suddenly, a white bird that had somehow gotten into the church started zooming around the upper zone of the nave. The kids were all staring up at the bird in rapt attention, and Father Sullivan, pointing up at the bird, quickly cashed in on the religious teaching opportunity.

"See children, that's my mother's soul flying to heaven," he said with the first –and last- smile I was ever to see on his face. Then the bird, either sick or disoriented, flew into a stained-glass window and dropped straight down to the floor. There was a loud gasp of horror from the congregation, and I thanked God that I was no longer a religion teacher and would have to the answer the students' questions when they returned to the school on why Father Sullivan's dead mother's soul ended up out cold on the tiles.

Three of the teachers began their careers at St. Dymphna's in, I think, the year of the flood. They called themselves "dinosaurs" and I hardly concurred with their assessment. The time spent at or monthly teacher meetings were extended by at least an extra hour as they added their unsolicited opinions by citing how things were done at the school half a century earlier. Set in their ways, they refused to bend to assist anyone. The yearly schedule had to be set to suit their whims. They hogged every hallway bulletin board. Even when they had nothing to show, they would put up a sign saying something was coming soon so that no other teachers could display their students' work. Although parking spaces were not assigned, nor were chairs at the table in the teachers' lounge, anyone who dared put their car or butt in one that they considered theirs by eminent domain faced a severe tongue lashing. It was little wonder that the rest of the teachers would rush to the Christmas luncheon every year to be able to sit as far from them as the length of the table would allow.

Because one of the dinosaurs was a nun, one an ex-nun, and the other connected with some big politician in the city, they were collectively treated as sacred cows. Mr. Thomas had actually been taught by the nun, and he unconsciously and automatically straightened his tie whenever she came into view. Although parents would complain at the periodically cruel treatment being dished out to their kids- pinching, poking, and tripping included-incidents were quickly hushed up.

Finally, tormented fourth-grade students took matters into their own hands to take down the most detested of the dinosaurs.

Mrs. Magma could have been the poster child for what not to do to be a good teacher. Her uninspiring instruction consisted of boring, then screaming at and berating, the students the entire day. The less than lavish decorations in her classroom consisted of four little faded fall leaves that stayed up through all seasons and holidays, year after year, decade after decade. The atmosphere in the room was an extension of her own personality- puritanical and dull.

Passing by her classroom during the Christmas parties one year, I saw Mrs. Magma, dressed (appropriately for her) in a red sweatshirt with the Grinch on it, bending over the desk of a terrified boy and, hatred burning in her eyes, screaming at him fiercely. Thinking what a great Christmas card it would make, I cursed myself for not carrying the camera from my classroom.

With scenes like these occurring daily, parents pulled their children out of the school, either before they entered the fourth grade or, after the kids had a dreadful year, right after they finished it. One situation spoke volumes when a parent took their child out of the school for his fourth grade year only.

The fourth graders had had enough, and they decided to take matters into their own little hands. Aware that Mrs. Magma had a habit of leaning on a student's desk while talking, one wily kid sensed an opportunity and pushed the desk out from under her. She crashed to the ground, landing directly on her bony old knees, to the total delight and cheering of the class. Mrs. Magma was carted off in an ambulance, never recovered completely from her fall, and was forced to retire. The boy who pushed the desk always claimed that it was an accident, but the gossip among the fourth graders at the water fountain gave him hero status because he had "gotten rid of the Magma." Her sudden departure was mourned by none.

Every year as Christmas approached, I would show my sixth grade homeroom the movie *The Bells of St. Mary's* and tell them that it had been filmed at the school. The church in the movie looked the same and the classroom building resembled the old school structure that was torn down in the 1960s when the existing one replaced it. To make the viewing even more interesting, I told them that one of the nuns at the school (the nice one, Sister Veronica) played the lead role in the film and was cast because she was a nun, so she already knew how to act like one. She went along with the ruse and, by some miracle, the students believed it. "She still says the same things and acts the same way today," was the consensus among them. When the nasty old nun, Sister Fatima, found this out, she was furious with me for not saying that she was the star of the movie. With her wizened looks and sour disposition, the only old movie character she could have played was the Wicked Witch in *The Wizard of Oz*, and the students would have believed it with no miracle required.

While teaching one of the kids' favorite topics, the Salem witch trials, I enlightened them with my childhood experiences in the Italian neighborhood of my youth. There, people still believed in the *malocchio*- the evil eye- and feared the *mamadels*, old widows dressed in black with canes, crosses, and grey buns whose husbands had died decades ago. *Mamadels,* it was thought, had the power to inflict harm on others with a penetrating stare. My great-grandmother had been trained in the ritual to remove the curse, and I remembered women coming to her, hand on head and lamenting, "Madonna, the headache." She would fill a bowl with water, pour oil on top, make the sign of the cross on the oil, say the secret words (these words could only be passed on to others in a dark bedroom at the stroke of midnight on Christmas Eve), and the curse was magically lifted.

One morning, upon returning from Sister Fatima's computer class (the kids hated going there, as she routinely bored, berated, and jabbed them with a bony finger), one boy, Harold, came back holding his head, his face twisted in pain.

"What's wrong?" I questioned, concerned.

"I have a terrible headache. I think Sister Fatima gave me the evil eye. Can I go to the office?"

"I don't think that she could do that," I said, suddenly reluctant to have him inform his parents that Mr. Consorte's lesson plan for the day consisted of a lecture on the evil eye and then, for cross subject reinforcement, Sister Fatima cursed him with it.

"Yes, she could. She's mean, and she looks just like one of those *mamadellas* you told us about," he replied, still holding the side of his head.

"Well, pray to Saint Teresa of Jesus, and if she doesn't want to help you, then go to the office and they'll take care of it. And forget the evil eye, it's all nonsense," I said smiling, trying to make light of the matter.

A half-hour later, the victim of unanswered prayers, Harold went to the office and returned after being given an aspirin. Thank God I never got an angry call from his parents on the matter. But maybe

Harold was not imagining things, for if anyone on earth could actually give an evil eye, and take a perverse pleasure in doing so, it was surely Sister Fatima.

I found it easier now to deal with nutty teachers as I had a year of basic training in that subject at Our Lady of The Holy Rosary Beads and had learned the tricks of the trade. Pay them perfunctory courtesy and avoid the teachers' lounge if possible as it was generally a breeding ground for hatred and revenge. The one thing teaching at the other school didn't prepare me for was dealing with students that spanned the entire range of learning challenges and personality disorders.

At this time, the archdiocese began closing schools left and right. The enrollment at many of the schools had dropped precipitously over the years as neighborhood demographics had changed. As one of the conditions to keep a school open was enough enrollment to make it self-supportive, all that a potential student needed to have to be admitted to the school was a pulse and the ability to pay the tuition, the latter being the more important of the two.

Having had less than no training in Special Education, I found myself with students afflicted with ADHD, Asperger's, Tourette Syndrome, severe learning disabilities (which, years ago, was just called stupid), and bi-polar disorders. The teachers were charged with the impossible task of getting them to all do well- or at least pass. Sister Veronica summed the situation up when she stated to me sadly, "I can't give them what God didn't."

We did the best we could with the resources (almost nothing) at our disposal. The severe cases were heavily medicated, and you could always tell when they forgot to take the correct dosage or when the drug was rapidly wearing off. My student with Tourette's was a sweet kid who loved, of all things, Frank Sinatra music, so whenever he seemed troubled or anxious, I tried a little experiment. I would play "That's Life," "Come Fly with Me," and other Sinatra songs. It worked! He would become calm and instantly return to task.

Steven was a quiet student with a relatively harmless, but disconcerting, quirk. He liked to chew on the corners of his books and would contentedly gnaw away through each class. Rather than have his books ruined, I bought him a doggie chew toy that resembled a hamburger and let him chew to his heart's content. For sanitary reasons, I washed it at the end of each school day and stored it in my desk.

Another student had a far more serious affliction, but I found a solution during, of all things, a lesson on Japan. Jacob's father was a crazy, violent criminal who was currently incarcerated. That fact in and of itself wasn't so unusual, as other students had parents in prison and would have family road trips once a month to visit them upstate. What I found fascinating was that Jacob's mother knew the father was schizophrenic, yet she thought it fine to marry him and have a kid. The result was Jacob, who had to be so heavily medicated that he appeared at times to be almost in a trance.

While talking about Japanese customs, somehow the topic of geisha girls came up. Just then, Mr. Chin entered the classroom to drop off a textbook one of the students had left in his room. Because he was raised in Asia and had first-hand knowledge of the area (the students loved his story of how he had to watch his uncle eat the brains of a live monkey), I asked him to tell them about the geishas.

"They wear lovely silk dress," he said, smiling and smoothing the sides of his legs with his hands. "And they perform beautiful tea service," he continued, making the gesture of delicately pouring a cup of tea.

"I heard they're hookers," one boy rudely called out.

"End of lesson. Come back next year," said Mr. Chin as he scurried from the room. Shifting topics swiftly, I showed the students the scene from *Godzilla* where the monster gleefully destroys downtown Tokyo. His fire-breathing antics were such a hit, I decided to stick with the genre and show the scene from *Mothra* in which doll-sized girls sing to call their super god, a giant moth, from captivity, referring to the flying monster as their guardian angel (religious art presents Catholic guardian angels in a much more attractive light).

I couldn't help but notice that the song, for some strange reason, had an acute calming effect on the previously agitated Jacob, as his facial features softened and his gaze drifted angelically upward toward the heavens above. From that day forward, whenever Jacob began acting out, signaling the fact that he had either forgotten to take his medication or it had worn off, I would play the *Mothra* song and the lion would turn into a lamb. We took this therapy to a higher level when I had the art teacher make me a large papier-mâché brown moth that I would hang from the ceiling over Jacob when the soothing song played.

This strange scene reached its zenith one morning when Sister Veronica, from the classroom next door, wandered to my room, lured by the music, and started happily singing along to the song. After it ended, she explained that she saw the movie as a kid and remembered the song. Who would have ever thought?

An outward eye looking upon this scene would probably think they were watching the final frames of a surrealistic film, as there stood an old Irish nun singing the lyrics to a song from a Japanese horror film while one boy munched a chew-toy and another

228

sat perfectly still under a large paper moth. But after a few years of teaching at St. Dymphna's, it seemed like just another mundane day to me.

Adding to all this nonsense was the janitor, Jose, whose idea of school maintenance was only to empty the wastebaskets in the classrooms at the end of the day. Although everyone complained of the crummy conditions, nothing changed. Jose had some sort of connection with the monsignor, I was told, so he wouldn't be fired. Plus, he was big and burly, covered with tattoos, and had a bad temper, so everyone was terrified of him. He referred to himself as a family man, the definition in his case being that he had two daughters by two different women, neither of which he married or supported. In all seriousness, he once complained to me that his ungrateful daughters had bought him cheap underwear from the Dollar Store for Fathers' Day and he was embarrassed to wear them on a date.

I just stared, not able to muster a spark of sympathy.

Unable to face the filth every day and fearful that we would be closed by the Board of Health, I came in early every morning to clean the school and pick up litter outside, hoping my fellow teachers and the higher ups might take a hint and come down on the janitor to do a better job. Instead, Mr. Thomas bought me tool with a point at the tip for picking up trash, and Sister Veronica presented me with a broom decorated with a big red bow for Christmas. The students who witnessed the gift giving were in agreement that it had to be the worst Christmas present of all time.

Chapter 12

Spare the Rod, Spoil the Child

D espite the school being in an awful, crime infested area, most of the students and classes were quite good. And then there was the class seemingly sent from the Devil down below, the group every grade level teacher dreaded getting the next year (not them, not them!). When they were in the fifth grade, I strolled by their classroom door after dismissal and saw their teacher, a lovely and dedicated young lady who would do anything to help her students, seated at her desk staring moodily at nothing.

She had assembled a witty fall display in the hall in front of her classroom. The phrase "It's not corny to study" was surrounded by ears of corn. One of the boys in her class had changed the wording to "It's not corny to stud" and drew dick heads on the ears of corn. Other classmates ratted out the culprit, as they always do, and he promptly received a suspension for the next day.

"Is something wrong, Janice?" I inquired, concerned by her depressed and defeated expression as she usually appeared so cheerful.

"I just don't like them," she said sorrowfully, and I understood completely. As a teacher, you want to like all the students, and you hope to change the miscreants for the better, but this group took kindness as an expression of weakness and were behaving toward her accordingly.

The next year when I got them for a homeroom, they were twelve going on twenty-two, nasty, and totally unlikeable. But they met their match with me, although that year made the trials of Job seem like a day at the beach.

There were a few good kids thrown in with that group and I felt sorry for them, as they were consistently either ignored or bullied by the hardcore clique.

One nice boy was both polite and an excellent student, two qualities that damned him in the eyes of the gang of miniature male thugs in the class. I separated the four boys that made up that gang by seating them in the four corners of the classroom, as far as possible from one another.

I couldn't follow them throughout the school, though, and the bullying took place outside my viewing range. Within a few weeks, the mother pulled the bullied boy out of the school and I lost the best student in that class.

The school held several holiday boutiques throughout the year to raise money. The students were allowed into the boutiques one class at a time to view and, hopefully, purchase the cheap merchandise. This class of miscreants would buy next to nothing, and yet after they departed, or, shall we say, made good their escape, many items were noticeably missing. They exhibited no shame or remorse when they were finally banned by the principal from future boutiques.

Even things belonging to the two nuns weren't off limits to these thieves, as nothing was sacred to them. Both Sisters found money missing from their handbags after these kids were in their classrooms. I wasn't at all surprised to overhear them planning to get together one Saturday to go Christmas shoplifting.

In an ironic twist to their holiday stealing spree, there was a shootout in the parking lot of the shopping center where their seventh commandment-breaking pilfering was taking place. When they ducked under a car for safety, the fat one got stuck and the others had to pull him out. At the class Christmas party, I played *"I'm gettin' nuttin for Christmas, 'cause I ain't been nuttin' but bad,"* as that song seemed to be made to order for this crew.

Their thieving ways hit an apex on the day Sister Veronica was sick and had to be taken from the school in an ambulance. A half hour before the students entered the building in the morning, she collapsed in the hallway and couldn't get up. When an ambulance arrived, it was accompanied by a fire truck. We were told by an upset Mr. Thomas to reroute the kids through another doorway so that they wouldn't see Sister Veronica lying flat out on the floor. When the students settled down in the classroom, I informed them a problem with Sister Veronica was the reason for the emergency vehicles and the reason they came in through a different door.

"Is she on fire?" asked one silly student.

"Of course not, she's just sick and had to go to the hospital," I said, noticing that one girl had brought in a CD player. No electronics were allowed in the school, but with all the other excitement that morning, I just let it go.

At the end of the day, I heard a shriek of horror and then hysterical sobbing coming from the coat closet at the rear of the room. Cindy, the girl who had brought in the CD player, explained between sobs that someone had stolen it.

She had put it on the shelf in the closet with her books and now it was gone.

"It's not mine, it's my brothers. He's going to kill me when he finds it missing," Cindy wailed, frightened.

I wanted to upbraid her for being so stupid as to bring something of value into grabbing distance of this nest of thieves, but it was too late for that, and finding out who committed the crime and recovering the stolen item took top priority at the moment.

"All right, which of you took Cindy's CD player?" I asked sternly, after searching the shelves myself.

Of course, I got no response, or even a nervous look.

"Get your backpacks and put them on your desks. Each of you is going to empty them out in front of me and no one is leaving this room until I've gone through every one of them," I commanded, the maniacal look on my face showing that I meant business.

The students, realizing that this was no joke, complied and raced en mass to the closet without complaint to get their belongings. In the middle of all the confusion the missing CD player miraculously reappeared. Of course, no one would admit to taking it. I had my suspicions but no proof, and, for once, there was honor among thieves. No one would rat out the culprit. So, to this day, the case of the missing CD player remains unsolved, and the culprit has probably progressed to grand larceny.

Their next little endeavor managed to get some of these students suspended. While riding home on the school bus, they thought it would be fun to scream out the open windows "fuck you" while giving the finger to people on the sidewalk. Eventually, they picked on the wrong person who, infuriated, tried to board the bus, yelling that he was going to kill them. The bus driver, scared half to death, reported the incident to Mr. Thomas, who duly suspended the guilty students the next morning. With them gone, I was treated to one of the most stress-free days that year.

As bad as some of the boys were, a few of the girls were worse. The three that were the ringleaders of many misdeeds were referred to privately by Mr. Chin and I as the "Macbeth witches" as they were always circled together, plotting some evil. All that was missing was a boiling cauldron and some eye of newt. When one of the boys annoyed them, they thought nothing on grabbing his crotch and squeezing hard, with the shocked teacher, unfortunately me, as a witness being no deterrent to them at all. The worst-case scenario was having to watch a girl with a twisted face that could stop a train performing this tender gesture on a two hundred-pound boy whose eyes almost popped out of his head. Reporting this heinous act to the principal did no good as the girls got a talking to and no more. So, I had to take the disciplining into my own hands.

How do you get monsters to do what you want? You could change their DNA, but that would take far longer than the length of one school year. Or you could make them stay in at recess, torturing them with a video of Tammy Faye Bakker singing "We Are Blessed" over and over again. Tiny Tim wouldn't do at St. Dymphna's. I knew that I needed to drag in the heavy artillery.

"What's wrong with her eyes?" one of the girls demanded to know.

"She's got a whole tube of mascara on them, that's what's wrong," I answered. Tammy Faye's singing did the trick, and the crotch grabbing, at least in my presence, was curtailed, to the vast relief of the boys.

One girl in that crass class, Daniella, was beyond boy crazy. With ample encouragement on her part, the boys were all over her, even in church. During one Mass, the response was, "The Lord hears the cry of the poor." The boys never made the responses unless threatened with dire punishment, and, even then, only in a barely audible whisper. Yet here they were, responding loudly and enthusiastically, the reason being they had substituted the word "whore" for "poor" while laughing and pointing to Daniella. To my horror, she seemed to enjoy even this misplaced attention.

I kept changing Daniella's seat in the classroom, but no matter where I put her there was a boy nearby to play with. When I found a note on the floor next to her desk rating the boys in the class from 1 to 10, I thought I had struck gold. One boy, Steven, received a 0 on her scale, along with the nasty notation "monkey face" next to his name. Steven was extremely shy and quiet, totally not her type. Or so I thought. I seated her next to him, hoping to throw a very wet blanket on her predatory nature. Didn't happen. In less than a week, even Steven began to look like a hunk to her. I conceded defeat and figured all I could do was keep a keen eye on her flirtatious activities and hope for the best.

However, Daniella cast her net beyond the confines of the classroom. Her mother raced into the office screaming one morning after discovering that Daniella had men in their twenties calling her during schooldays on her cellphone. That explained all her desperate trips to the girls' room. I had been told never to deny a girl in middle school a bathroom request, for obvious reasons, but Daniella's were now suddenly few and far between. Despite all precautions, I wasn't surprised when she had to suddenly leave before the end of the school year and live with relatives in the mid-west.

By far the most upsetting incident of that annoying year was a severe case of bullying by a cruel group of girls and their conspiracy against me when I tried to stop it. If they had succeeded in their machinations, my teaching career would have terminated that year, and I could have ended up behind bars.

Bullies always seem to be able to scent someone who won't fight back, and that's who they target and attack. In this case, it was a none-too-bright classmate of theirs. Sonjay was a sweet kid, one of the few in that class, hence she didn't fit in at all with the mean clique of girls. They made fun of her looks, which was a joke as none of them were beauty contest material. They also ridiculed her grades, her lack of friends in the class, and anything else they could come up with. In the cafeteria, where the students were allowed to sit only with others in their grade, Sonjay sat alone at the far end of the table, weeping while the others refused to talk to her.

It was killing me to watch this nasty nonsense, and I helped Sonjay by moving her seat in the classroom next to a girl whose company she enjoyed, as well as letting her sit with another class in the cafeteria. Somewhat foiled in their plans to torment Sonjay to death, they were out for my blood.

I had reported this blatant case of bullying to Mr. Thomas many times, but my warnings fell on deaf ears. He had many concerns, having to deal with crazy parents, teachers, students, and threats of lawsuits at the moment, so my problem seemed trivial. Then, one day, the situation exploded.

Sonjay had composed a well-written, heartfelt letter describing the harassment and, because of it, her hatred of her tormenters and intense dislike of the school. It was hand delivered to Mr. Thomas in his office by Sonjay's screaming mother. After he calmed her down and she departed for her job, he hurried down to my classroom, called me out into the hallway, and showed me the letter. I was shocked. Not at the content of the letter, but by the fact that it was so well written.

It was on the tip of my tongue to blurt out "I told you so," but it would have been rude and, after all, he was my boss. Plus, he knew I had come to him several times with this problem, and he probably now regretted ignoring it. He stormed past me into my classroom and I shadowed him, eager to watch the drama I was sure to come. I wasn't disappointed.

He railed at those girls in a justified fit of righteous anger, combining shock at their rotten behavior with threats of retaliation if it continued. The girls involved just looked at him impassively, not at all ashamed at what they did and annoyed that they would now be more closely monitored. The bullying stopped after that, but, because they blamed me for cutting short their "fun," the witches huddled together ominously, and their revenge came swiftly.

The very next day, I was summoned to Mr. Thomas' office and the hideous blow fell. Without any formality, he got right to the point.

"Sit down, Jimmy," he said, and I, sensing something was very wrong, sank into the chair in front of his desk.

"Ashley, Joann, and Emerald were just in here and said that you touched Joann when she bent over the water fountain. Don't get upset, because I realize they are probably just retaliating after my talk to them yesterday, but I still have to investigate this."

Don't get upset! I fought a valiant battle for self-control, trying to make my emotions quiet as I realized the enormity of the accusations and the awful consequences because of them. My heated denials began, but Mr. Thomas quickly silenced me and told me his plan.

"I'm calling their mothers in here one by one, and I will have the girls come in also. I want to see what they have to say in front of them and you. In the meantime, act like nothing has happened."

That would be easier said than done, but I sensed what he was up to, and I had no other choice anyway. So, I went back to the classroom and, by sheer force of will, assumed an air of cheerful nonchalance. The performance deserved an Academy Award.

Mr. Thomas was as good as his word. Each of the girls was called to his office and found her mother

already waiting there. I was sent for while one of
the office ladies watched whatever class I had at the
time, and each girl was greeted by a grim tribunal
consisting of their principal, mother, and me. Each
scenario played out the same way. The liar would cry,
confess she made the story up, and blame the other
two girls for putting her up to it. None would meet
my eyes when they were forced to apologize.

And that was the end of it. There were no
detentions or suspensions, much less expulsions. I
suppose I should have been happy it ended there,
but I was far from it, and I endured a totally sleepless
night wondering how I could possibly face those
demon seeds for the next two years, much less teach
them. Plus, by not punishing them in any way, what
kind of a life lesson was the school, a Catholic school
at that, providing them with? It was a situation that
would leave a scar on my soul for years to come.

"*Behold, you are angry, and we are sinful;*
all of us have become like unclean people,
all our good deeds are like polluted rags;
we have withered like leaves," read Ashley
reluctantly. I had picked her to do the afternoon
prayer the next day and searched for one I thought
fitting for the occasion, not caring if the analogies and
meanings would be lost on most of the class.

"*and our guilt carries us away like the wind.*
There is none who calls upon your name,

who rouses himself to cling to you:
for you have hidden your face from us
and have delivered us up to our guilt
The word of the Lord," finished Ashley with a
smirk.

"Thanks be to God," responded the students
whom the reading didn't refer to. On the last day
of school, I usually played Roy Rogers and Dale
Evans singing "Happy Trails to You," but when this
homeroom group made its exit that year, I played
Chopin's "Funeral March."

Two years later, when this class graduated, I would
have paid good money not to attend the ceremony. I
informed Mr. Thomas of my feelings and said that I
was only going out of respect for him. He replied that
he understood and thanked me. I wasn't alone in my
feelings, as this batch of brats weren't exactly beloved
by the other teachers as they had behaved in an awful
manner with all of them. When Ashley got up to get
her diploma, Sister Veronica, seated next me in a pew,
leaned over to me and hissed, "Boo, boo." That bit of
comic relief helped get me through the ceremony, and
the instant it was over I ducked out a side door of the
church and raced off in my car. I was already down
the street when I saw the first people emerging from
the large front doors. In an act of complete sacrilege,
I gave the finger under the dashboard. I knew it was a

common, childish, crude gesture, but it made me feel better.

Despite all this, the years I spent at St. Dymphna's were generally happy ones, much better than the time at my previous post, where I had been cast beyond the reach of hope.

Then came a round of school closings. One poor teacher had the misfortune to be in three closing schools in the past five years. Not surprisingly, we hoped he would never darken the door of St. Dymphna's, as he was considered, perhaps unfairly, the harbinger of death. But even without his presence we were doomed, as the monsignor had no interest in the school and would much prefer to receive the money every year for its rental to the city.

We were aware of his mercenary desire, yet during the staff meeting at the beginning of the year, he appeared before us to announce that he had been assured by the higher-ups in the archdiocese that St. Dymphna's was not on the hit list of schools to close that year. The schools to close would be notified in October. We all breathed an audible sigh of relief and continued the meeting, planning the great things we wanted to accomplish that year.

But the euphoria was to be short lived.

It was on the day of Sister Camillus' funeral that the hideous blow fell. A very old woman, Sister Camillus lived in the nun's retirement home close to the school. During the last years of her life, she would hobble into the school on surprise visits to talk to the students about Mother Seton. The problem was, she would forget that she talked to the same class just the day before and would return, unannounced, for an unwelcome encore. And her timing couldn't have been worse. She always seemed to appear just when we were in the middle of preparing the students for a big test the next day, or attempting to get through the day's lesson because the homework assignment was based on it.

Her entrance was announced by the aluminum leg of a walker appearing at the threshold of the classroom door. Five minutes after that, the rest of her would be inside. Eons later, she would leave. Once, an announcement came over the PA system asking for a student to come to the office. Of course, all hands went up as everyone in the room leaped at the opportunity to get out of the class for a while.

"Gabriel, you can go," I said, picking one of the better students, and he leaped up from his chair.

Then came the rest of the request, "Sister Camillus needs someone to help her to the church." Gabriel's gait came to a screeching halt and he began to head back to his chair as the kids started laughing.

"Too late," I told him, smiling. "You volunteered, so go, and we'll see you next year."

When she died, we attended an all-school Mass during which the monsignor went through a litany of her many virtues.

"And her last words were, 'Make sure there is five dollars in my envelope for Sunday's collection,'" he concluded. Then her casket was pushed down the aisle at a speed faster than she had experienced in years and we filed back to our classrooms with mixed emotions, sorry for her demise but secretly relieved by the reprieve from the repetitious, tired tale of Mother Seton's life.

Chapter 13

We Followers of Our Suffering Lord are Marching to the Tomb

"If you had to go to the outhouse or the woods to go to the bathroom, you would say, 'I have to pluck a rose,' which was a lot prettier than saying what you really had to do," I explained to an interested audience in the middle of my lesson on colonial hygiene. Holding up a chamber pot, I was about to continue when the secretary from the office, looking like she just saw death, appeared at my door.

"Mr. Thomas would like to see you, Mr. Consorte," she said sadly. "I'll watch your class until you get back."

It was October, and despite the reassuring words from the monsignor, I sensed, though I tried not to believe, the reason I was being summoned.

"So, the monsignor lied to us," I said, miffed after being told what I expected to hear.

"I don't know if he really knew or not," replied Mr. Thomas truthfully. "There will be a team coming from the archdiocese in November to go over everything with us. We'll have more information then. That's all I know."

There was no point in a display of either sorrow or anger. It wouldn't have changed the situation, and, after all, Mr. Thomas was in the same boat. A worse one, actually, as he had a family to support. I slowly returned, almost zombie-like, to the classroom, said nothing to the students concerning the demise of the school, and continued my lecture on the chamber pot, explaining how people used to dump then out of second-story windows on the people in the street below. I thought to myself that the people on the receiving end must have felt pretty much the same as the principals, teachers, staff workers, parents, and students in the scores of unlucky Catholic schools that were cast out in the cold that day.

And so began the sad process of observing and participating in the slow death of a school that had been the mainstay of a neighborhood for the past century, as well as feeling the torment of rising and falling hope regarding the future. Principals from the schools that were staying open were forced to hire teachers from the closing schools before considering any other applicants. There was a list based on seniority, so those with the longest time teaching in the archdiocese had the best shot at an opening for another job. Some would retire, others would seek jobs in public schools, but the vast majority prayed for deliverance within the archdiocese. Some prayers would be answered, and the saints would turn a deaf ear to others.

Everything we did that year, the holiday celebrations, class trips, and ceremonies, all took on a morbid meaning as we knew they were happening for the last time. It didn't help that I had one of the best homerooms ever and would have loved to have taught those students for the next two years. An exaggerated example of my high esteem for them was when we had a colonial tavern party where we would only have foods used in colonial times. They had never tasted gingerbread, so I baked some for the party. I don't cook anything - period! For me to have actually shopped for ingredients and made some form of food was a supreme sacrifice. They liked it so much (Lord knows why) that I made it once every week for them during the rest of that year. And I haven't cooked a damn thing since.

Despite this dire situation, puberty, with its raging hormones, had no holiday among the seventh graders. Some of the girls would tease the boys and, when they responded, the coquettes would suddenly turn coy and scream, "Don't touch me!" Seeing where this was headed, I reluctantly decided to have a talk with the boys before something bad occurred. We had enough problems already.

"Listen up," I began in a warning tone to the assembled group of horny thirteen-year-olds. "I can see what's going on. If you touch these girls inappropriately, you can get in big trouble and have your lives ruined. Even if they like you, they can turn on you for any reason and accuse you of touching them in the wrong way, or worse!" I was beating around the bush, being uncomfortable with this whole subject, but the boys were far from naïve and my meaning was crystal clear.

"You mean I can never touch a girl again?" one boy, Jerry, who looked about eight years old, wailed. "My life is over," he lamented, dramatically dropping his head to the desk and covering it with his arms.

"I didn't say you could never touch a girl," I said, sensing the dilemma that was surly coming.

"I'm just telling you what can happen if you do. If a girl accuses you of inappropriate behavior, she won't get into trouble and you will," I went on, groping for words. "What you do outside of the school is your and your parents' business, but here, the teachers are responsible for you, so hands off. You can touch them all you want after you marry them," I finished, thinking this was good Catholic advice.

After that, either the teasing girls lost some of their lust or the boys got better at hiding their curious adolescent hands, but at least we didn't have an incident in the school that year. What went on outside the school that concerned the students I didn't know or honestly care, as there were far too many other pressing problems at the moment.

Insanity among certain members of the teaching staff didn't take a break that last year and lasted to the bitter end.

One afternoon, Mr. Thomas was in his office following dismissal, the mid-term report cards spread out on his desk, when his computer acted up. Jean, a teacher who knew something about computers, offered to take a look at it. She was seated at the computer, attempting to solve the problem, when Sister Fatima, who taught computers, although she knew next to nothing about them, came into the office, quickly summed up the situation, and ordered Jean away from the computer so she could take over. Jean refused, which enraged Sister Fatima, who raced over to Jean and sunk her nails into her shoulders, forgetting, or not caring, that Jean was an adult and not one of her students.

"Take your fucking hands off me!" screamed Jean, who jumped out of the seat and headed for the door, wisely thinking that if she stayed in the room fists might begin to fly.

Mr. Thomas, a horrified witness to the scene, and aware that there could be parents of students outside his door, begged for peace. "Ladies, please!" he implored, quickly standing up and holding out his arms in an age-old gesture of appeal.

Jean was just about to escape out the door when Sister Fatima, seeing her prey getting away, took the glass of water that was near the computer table and flung the contents across Mr. Thomas' desk at Jean.

Spotting what was about to happen, Mr. Thomas, arms still outstretched, screamed "Nooooooo!" and fell flat on his desk in a valiant effort to protect the report cards. He received a soaking back for his effort. Sister Fatima then chased Jean down the hall, but Jean made it to her classroom and locked the door just in the nick of time. From that moment on, the two of them didn't talk to each other, badmouthed each other to anyone who would listen, and, at the last luncheon, sat surrounded by their warring camps at the north and south poles of the table.

And that luncheon came only too soon. When we first got notice in October that the school was closing, June seemed far off. Then, suddenly, it was here. It was an enormous amount of physical work to pack up a school, as everything had to be completely cleaned out of the classrooms and either thrown out, given away, or carted home. This somber task was performed with the same amount of enthusiasm displayed when taking down a Christmas tree or closing up a summer home, when you sense that what is coming in the near future won't be as satisfying as what is now being left behind.

The eighth-grade graduation was particularly poignant as it was to be the end of an era. Mr. Thomas and the teachers tried to be cheerful for the sake of the students, as it was there big day, but it was hard to hold back the tears. At least the monsignor didn't ruin the ceremony. Earlier in the year, he had told the students that the school was closing because they didn't go to church often enough on Sundays, which was a lie and served no purpose but to make them feel badly. It was a blessing that he was on his best behavior.

The ending of the graduation ceremony had everyone in the church singing and the church bells chiming to the same tune, as had happened countless times before. Then the final note sounded. It was over forever.

But there was still another week of school before the rest of the students left. Some teachers had already received calls for interviews at other schools. I had received a call myself, and the principal scheduled an interview with me at her school on the Monday after the last day of school. It would be a much longer and more difficult commute, but it was a job and the principal seemed very nice.

Every year at this time, the history teachers had to give the eighth-grade state exam. Whoever first deemed that the exam be given this late in the term either never entered a classroom toward the end of a school year or was a dyed in the wool sadist. In their minds, the eighth graders were already out of the school and couldn't care less about a state test, and the teachers had to scramble to correct these exams at the busiest time of the year. Delicacy forbids me from repeating the teachers' comments regarding the year-end state tests.

I had been tapped for the past couple of years to help correct the tests. The teachers chosen, along with some principals in charge, were assembled in the gym of a Catholic school, provided with bagels, muffins, and coffee (the best part of the day), and were given instructions on what to do. Then piles of tests were put on our table and we dug in. One interesting point was seeing the academic strengths or weaknesses of students from the other schools, making you either wish you had them in your classes or glad you were spared.

This year, the principal in charge instructed us to let her see every test that was receiving a failing grade. I got the hint. The grade on the last portion of the test, the essay, was up to the corrector's discretion, although there were strict guidelines to go by. I never gave anyone one point more than the guidelines demanded, as it wasn't worth losing your job if you got caught. But as long as this principal's initials were on the better grades, I was off the hook. So, I obediently handed over all the failing exams to her and wondered if she was capable of miracles, as she would need a few to suddenly produce written answers from blank pages.

Finally, the last day of school arrived, and with it the sensation of being put out of one's long misery. I arrived at my classroom with the fixed intention of looking toward the future, rather than being bothered with the past, and dealing with the events of the day in a mature, manly manner. The students had their classroom farewell parties, received their report cards, and everything seemed almost normal.

I lined the students up for the last time and led them to the door to the school yard. Then, without warning, it happened. The closer I got to the door, the harder the lump in my throat became. I made it to the glass doors and was greeted by a sea of sorrow. Mr. Thomas, the teachers, the students, and the parents were all out in front of the school in tears. My students filed out slowly, each turning to me to say a last goodbye, which became increasingly difficult to return. Carlos was the last to leave. It was his brother who was the first to enter the school and greet me on my first day. How strange, yet somehow fitting, that now his younger brother was presenting me with my final farewell. He didn't get a reply from me, but the look on my face told him why. I couldn't speak. Then I quickly returned to my classroom, closed the door so no one could see me, and bawled like a baby.

The next Monday morning at ten, I found myself entering the office of a chubby, cheerful principal named Sister Rita who had spotted me on the list of teachers that had to be hired and requested me to come for my interview. I spotted a picture of an *I Love Lucy* television episode on the wall and said, "I can tell you exactly what episode that scene is from. That is one of my all-time favorite TV shows."

"It's my favorite show too," she said, laughing. "You're hired." And thus began what had to be the best job interview since Joseph met with Pharaoh.

The rest of the interview, if you could even call it that, consisted of us talking about the TV shows and toys of our childhoods. During this trip down memory lane fun fest, she said that my credentials were impeccable and penned in an increase of four thousand dollars on the contract that I couldn't sign quickly enough. Then I was given a friendly, fun tour of the school and floated out to the parking lot on Cloud 9.

Ecstatic that I would still be teaching without even the loss of one paycheck, I called all of my co-workers from St. Dymphna's to tell them of my salvation and wish them the same. Then, two days later, I received a call from Sister Rita.

"Mr. Consorte, I'm so sorry to have to tell you this," she began in a very embarrassed voice. "There were other teachers on the list that I should have interviewed before you, so I'm afraid that you're not hired after all. Again, I'm really sorry and I wish you luck," she concluded, sincerely. Sister Rita hung up, and though, I didn't know it at the time, that was essentially the end of my career with the archdiocese. My next permanent teaching job would be over a thousand miles away, down among the sheltering palms.

A hot-headed man turns up strife, and there was absolutely nothing to be gained simmering because of Sister Rita's mistake as I didn't want to deter future interviews. She had only tried to do what Mrs. Devilica had done years before, hiring out of order, only she didn't get away with it. Also, I assumed that if it was that easy to get one job so quickly, other offers would soon follow.

But such was not the case. September came, the new school year started, and I was still stuck in the basement of the list. According to some of my colleagues who were hired, they were hardly welcomed with warm smiles and open arms by their new principals, who had resented having to hire them and, in certain cases, rudely told them so. They were set up to fail, given large classes full of crazy kids, and provided with no disciplinary support from their principals. Some rode it out in acute misery for the duration, much of their time spent in tears, while others ran for the exits before the ball descended to announce the new year.

All the kids from my last homeroom went to the same Catholic school just down the street from Saint Dymphna's. As Christmas approached, I called the principal there and asked if I could visit them. Understanding the situation, she said yes, and on a blustery winter morning the following week, I drove to the school in an upbeat mood, not realizing I was on a fool's errand, against all common sense.

My former students met me in the hallway outside the office during their recess. They looked the same, probably because they were dressed in Catholic school uniforms and little time had passed since I last saw them. We joked around as I presented them with Christmas cards and little gifts, and they seemed genuinely glad to see me. Then, all too soon, the bell rang, and they had to leave for their afternoon classes, so I wished them a merry Christmas and departed through the front door, trading the bustling, vibrant atmosphere of the school for the dreary, lonely winter afternoon. By the time I reached the car, the sweetness of remembering the past was suddenly as bitter as gall, and I drove home in tears, silently vowing never to visit them again.

The hiring list from the archdiocese stipulated that you could refuse two job offers but were then forced to take the third one or you would be kicked off the list forever. There was no point in taking a position that was fraught with so many pitfalls that you knew you wouldn't last. A dead giveaway that the offer was a stinker was insider knowledge that the teacher you would be replacing unceremoniously quit in the middle of the week. Over the course of a year, I had to turn down two offers because the principals wanted me to teach middle school math. I was no more capable of that than I was of jumping up and flying to the moon. I hadn't had a math course since the tenth grade, and I had hung on to a passing grade all year by my fingernails.

After turning down the two job offers that I couldn't do, even if someone held a gun to my head, so I got booted from the list. I realized that if I still wanted to work in the field of education at a Catholic school, it would have to be outside of the immediate area.

I sent some resumes to other areas of the country and soon received a call from an expensive, exclusive (or so I thought), private Catholic school in the wealthy town of Narcissus, on the east coast of Florida.

"We are very impressed with your resume. When can you come down for an interview?" questioned Mr. Cain, the assistant principal.

I made an airline reservation, booked a cheap rental car and an even cheaper motel room, and soon found myself in a lush area of Florida I had never visited before.

Chapter 14

The Righteous Will Flourish Like Palm Trees

I spent the day at the Garden of Eden School shadowing Mr. Cain, who turned out to be a wizened little man with a shock of hair the color of a carrot and the annoying habit of never looking into your eyes when he spoke to you. The school day began with him screaming some evangelical stuff to the assembled students. He continued preaching and pontificating before the bored group until I longed for the classes to begin. With all the moralizing and praying I realized that the mode of operation here was a far cry from that practiced in the archdiocese where I previously taught. But I figured a few extra acts of faith couldn't hurt anyone, as long as I didn't have to be the one to initiate them.

During the teaching of Mr. Cain's class, I had more secular warnings of what might be in store. His seating arrangement just screamed problems, as all the girls were seated together on one side of the room and the boys on the other, something I knew never worked. Predictively, the girls gabbed away with one another and pretty much ignored me.

Then something much more ominous occurred, which sent up warning rockets as to what working with Mr. Cain would be like. In an attempt at camaraderie, I had shared a story with him of an incident at a reenactment. Mr. Cain asked me to repeat the anecdote to the students for their amusement. Though the story was in somewhat questionable taste for kids, I complied, thinking if he thought it was okay, I was safe.

It backfired, of course, as some of the students started asking very pointed questions.

"Mr. Consorte told you about that, I didn't, in case your parents ask," Mr. Cain shouted in alarm, showing me right then and there that if he could shift blame for his actions to the detriment of others, he would, and without a second of hesitation.

Next, I was sent to the headmaster, Mrs. Marian, a lovely, middle-age lady, and was duly hired. All that was left to do was sell or rent my condo and move to Florida in five months. I signed the "at will" contract with little thought, carelessly casting aside the adage "be careful what you wish for, you may get it."

Just before leaving, I was in the office of a principal, Mrs. DePaulo, whom I had been a substitute teacher for after my unemployment ended.

She had been kind enough to let me use her as a reference and had spoken at length to Mr. Cain, who she thought was more than a little strange.

"Are you sure you know what you're doing?" she asked. "One of the things Mr. Cain kept asking me was how devout you are, so I'm sort of worried about what you may be in for."

"It's worth a try," I said with a sigh. "If I still want to teach, this is my opportunity. And if things don't go as planned, I can always come back to New York."

"Good luck, Jimmy," she said, with the inference that I would need it. "And start praying to Saint Denis."

There were three things I adamantly requested from the Florida real estate renting agent I dealt with. No one living above me, no annoying neighbors, and a relatively quiet environment. I didn't have much time to find a place, and I took what he suggested based on my needs. When I arrived at the beautiful condo complex after an almost deadly drive, being terrorized by tractor-trailers the entire way, I found the worst of all situations. There were noisy lowlifes living above me and a river only twenty feet from my lanai that was home to alligators, snakes, and possibly brain-eating amoebas. The river was swelling from torrential summer rains, leaving me, despite the suffocating heat, cold with fear that at some point soon it would come flooding into my home, carrying its assortment of deadly prehistoric creatures with it.

Then there was the nightmare of my belongings being in suspended animation. The moving company provided me with continuous lame excuses why everything I owned in the world had not gotten down there yet. All I had were the few pieces of clothing I had managed to cram into my car. And to make matters worse, when I mentioned my situation to people I met, I heard one horror tale after another of rip-off moving companies and customers losing all their worldly goods. I thanked the Lord on bended knee when the moving van arrived at long last over a month late.

The Garden of Eden School should have been named Garden of Evils as it sat in a poorly drained, swampy area and was surrounded by snakes, poisonous frogs, armadillos that could carry leprosy (how biblical), and, occasionally, a wandering bobcat or bear. The first week I was there, I was seated in the chapel for our morning prayers when I spotted a snake on the floor in front of me. A fierce, charging lion would have been preferable as I harbor an uncontrollable, intense fear of those slithering creatures. In the middle of the prayer service, I screamed "snake" and got up from my seat with the fixed intention of racing from the room, but one of the larger ladies, seated in the aisle next to me, blocked my escape route like a big boulder in the road.

"Move it!" I yelled, well beyond caring if the Pope was in the room. Her big butt stayed glued to the chair, so I climbed over her and took off, not stopping until I got to the safety of my classroom. I later learned that the science teacher took the black racer snake outside and casually tossed it into the swamp. This was the first but, unfortunately, far from the last of my encounters with the wildlife encircling and laying siege to the school.

My homeroom class had Mr. Cain as their teacher the previous year, so they were used to doing pretty much whatever they pleased, whenever they pleased, with impunity. The problems with that mode of operation are obvious. Little, if any, learning will take place, and, eventually, someone will become physically or mentally harmed. Then the question will be asked, as it always is, "Where was the teacher when this happened?" It didn't help the situation that some of the girls in the group and one of the boys had mild mental issues caused by unhappy home lives, fluctuating hormones, brain imbalances, or a lethal combination of all three. Tossed into this troublesome mix was a tough new student, Dana, with a very twisted family background that, rumor in the office had it, included so much alcohol addiction they could have opened their own clinic. The survival instinct within me sensed trouble and, hearing her in the hallway boasting to the other girls that she managed to get a male teacher fired at her school the year before, caused considerable concern and didn't exactly endear her to me. Nor did her passive-aggressive behavior, lying, sneakiness, and free hands with the other students.

One of her methods of annoyance was to put her head down into her folded arms on her desk to try to sleep through the class. I remembered the nun in catechism class who, if a student dared to do this, would get a water pistol out of her desk, sneak up on the culprit, and squirt him in the face. All I could do was threaten a demerit. Ah, the good old days of discipline. Later in the school year, she would pick on the wrong student and cause a nasty situation that would result in a threatened lawsuit by enraged parents.

Chapter 15

Holy Rollers and Jumpers They Come Out, and They Preach and They Jump and They Shout

Joe Hill

On the plus side, most of the teachers were friendly, supportive, and fun to be with. The exceptions were the ones who presented themselves as "holier than thou" and were cultish in their fanaticism. What amazed me the most about them was their cold, aloof, preachy attitudes and the ease in which lies sprang so readily from their lips. Unfortunately, none practiced the virtues that they preached.

Neither did they teach the students a basic religious rule: "Do unto others as you would have them do to you."

In fact, they reminded me of nothing more than a quote in a Tennessee Williams play: "Somebody said once or wrote: 'We are all children in a vast kindergarten, trying to spell God's name with the wrong alphabet blocks!'" But they went through the formalities of religion relentlessly, and the rest of the staff and the students were forced to follow suit. We had to sing songs like "This little light of mine" and "He's got the whole world in his hands". Not being a demonstrative person and used to a more sedate form of worship in my former schools, I found it difficult to adjust.

There was a prayer to begin each class (mine were short and sweet), a prayer to begin each meeting with a parent, and a prayer at the end of the day, although trying to keep students from sneaking out before performing it was a constant chore. But the longest and most poorly timed prayer was right after recess. The students were let loose to run around in the glaring noonday Florida sun for a half hour and then had to form up under a scorching, coppery sky, sweating profusely and dehydrating, for a three-minute prayer. Many kept track of the time and would use any plausible excuse to gain access to the air-conditioned buildings and the blessing of the water coolers just before recess ended. Big surprise, they didn't come back out. Unfortunately, all this excess praying was having the opposite effect on the students than intended.

"Who said, 'Give me liberty or give me death?'" I asked the seventh-grade class after just teaching the chapter on events leading to the American Revolution.

"George Washington," answered Andre.

"Nice try. It was Patrick Henry," I corrected him, and then tossed out an old figure of speech, "You get the booby prize." The students gasped in horror and looked at me like I had lost my mind.

"I'll take it," Kenny called out, smiling, while some of the other boys giggled. I grew increasingly uncomfortable, thinking that maybe they don't use that expression any longer and suddenly feeling very dated.

"A booby means a fool," I said, desperately trying to extricate myself from the uncomfortable situation. I was suddenly saved, not by the bell, but by a frog. It came leaping out of the classroom closet and the kids started screaming.

"I'll put him outside," said Kenny, quickly rising from his desk and racing over to the amphibian.

"Don't touch it, it could be poisonous," screamed some of the students.

"Mr. Consorte, don't let him touch it," pleaded one girl.

"Kenny will die," was the dire prediction of another. Meanwhile, the frightened frog was leaping all around the room and the students, seeking safety, stood on their chairs.

"Only cats die if they touch the poisonous kind," reassured another student, leaving me wondering where they were getting all this detailed amphibian information from. Then, suddenly, Keith grabbed the frog. I held my breath for a brief moment of horror, but Keith wasn't killed, either because the frog wasn't poisonous or Keith wasn't a cat.

Just a week after the frog incident, Larry, a third grade student, was helping me carry some things to my car. We were walking across a parking lot that was populated by a number of parents and kids when a long black snake came slithering out from under a car and crossed our path. We both ran screaming across the lot, the fear-crazed teacher outrunning the third grader and putting on quite a show for those watching. From that day on, I received an announcement from the office over the PA system whenever a snake was spotted on campus. But I already knew that snakes weren't the most dangerous creatures at the school.

By the third month into the school year, Dana was causing big problems, yet nothing was being done to curtail her bad behavior. Nor was there any feedback on her more than deserved demerits from me and the other teachers. When I overheard her tell another student, "Mr. Cain always takes my side," I knew that her impulsive, bullying behavior and loose hands, given free rein, would quickly lead to trouble, as she knew that she could behave as she pleased with impunity.

I warned Mr. Cain that I had seen this same scenario happen before and there was trouble on the way, but he brushed my warnings aside and assured me that he'd pray for her.

Her situation came to a head on "Grandparent's Day" when she grabbed one of the boys in my classroom.

"Mr. Consorte, Dana's touching me," Craig called out.

"I'll report it to Mr. Cain," was my quick reply, as I was busy exchanging pleasantries with a visiting parent.

Dana raced from the room and, a moment later, her grandmother, a big old bruiser from Bridgeport, Connecticut whose e-mail was, incongruously, "Butterfly," came charging in, screaming at me in the hallway in front of students and parents.

She was searching for Craig, declaring indelicately and loudly that she would "beat his skinny ass" when she found him.

"Come on, I'm ready for you," came the defiant voice of Craig from the sanctuary of my classroom, protected by the barrier of my body in the doorway between them. All I could think of at the moment was the irony of coming all the way to Florida only to be attacked by a lunatic who once lived close to my home in the northeast. But I had been through situations like this before (except that they were student vs. student, not student vs. shit-kicking grandma) and I knew that the best thing to do was stay calm, say as little as possible, and, eventually, the sound and the fury will abate.

After a moment of this standoff, "Butterfly" apologized, insisting I shake her hand, but the damage was done. Craig wisely said nothing, inwardly relieved that physical conflict was avoided as he probably sensed that he would have ended up as a human punching bag.

Later in the year, Dana pushed another girl into the bushes while walking between buildings. The injured student's parents had the police come to the school and wanted Dana charged with assault and battery. When they threatened a lawsuit, Dana was unceremoniously booted from the school.

Although Dana worried me, the real problem came from another student, Michelle, a miserable girl whose mother managed a bank. Angry that I wouldn't let her sit next to her friend and talk throughout my class, she sought her revenge. I always made it a point to stand at my classroom door and greet each student as they entered. When I said "Good morning" to Michelle, she gave me a cold glare and rudely paraded past me.

"I said good morning," was my answer to her disrespect, and she reluctantly mumbled a greeting without looking at me.

The next day, I was called into Mr. Cain's office. "Michelle said that you grabbed her when she didn't say hello to you," he said in a bland tone one would use to discuss the weather, not an accusation that could sound the death knell of a teacher's career. The words cut through me like a sharp blade.

"That is a bold-faced lie!" I said indignantly. "I've never touched her or any other student in my life. Call her mother in here right now," I demanded, beyond the point of caring what Mr. Cain, or anyone else, thought, being so thoroughly disgusted.

Mr. Cain summoned Michelle's mother, whose Mercedes pulled into the parking lot a half hour later. The expression on her face as she entered the office said "not again."

I didn't hurl accusations, although I would have loved to. I just denied what I had been accused of and she sighed and accepted the truth, saying that her daughter had lied to her before. I departed, somewhat mollified, but again, irreparable damage had been done. Plus, I never received an apology and had to look at Michelle's mean little face every day in my classroom.

"'Vengeance is mine, I will repay', says the Lord," I remembered. I was in no mood to wait around for that to happen, so I moved Michelle to a part of the classroom out of my major line of vision and placed a special education kid on each side of her. Have a nice life.

If you grew up in the northeast, it will never really feel like Christmas in Florida, no matter how many strands of lights are twisted around palm trees. I've always decorated my classroom with a 1950s theme for Christmas, complete with vintage decorations, bubble lights on the tree, and toys from my childhood. When the students' grandparents viewed the classroom, some were reduced to tears as they recognized items that they hadn't seen since childhood. I asked Mrs. Marian if I could come in on the Friday after Thanksgiving to complete the task of decorating. She gave her consent, as there would be a custodian there during the day. The fact that I would be there almost alone signaled a warning bell, especially considering all the misfortunes that had recently occurred, but the warning went unheeded.

The Connie Francis Christmas album was playing on my vintage record player when I moved a chair over to the shelf where I would display the old toys. I picked up a smiling, sharply dressed little rubber frog to place up on the shelf. Froggy was a character on *Andy's Gang*, a surreal Saturday morning children's TV show from the 1950s that was hosted by a highly inebriated Andy Devine. He would call, "Pluck

your magic twanger, Froggy" (to be interpreted in
a number of ways) to make Froggy appear. I looked
closely at Froggy, remembering the holiday I got him
from Santa and realizing how long ago that Christmas
morning was. Connie was singing "Ave Maria," which
I always thought beautiful, as I climbed up on a chair
to place Froggy on the shelf. Then, without warning, it
happened.

I fell off the chair, landing on one foot, which
twisted over. Suddenly I was on the floor, slowly
passing out from the intense pain, staring at the
blurred vision of Froggy, who had landed on the
floor in front of me. All I could think was, "This is
it, I'm dying. And what a stupid way to go, staring at
Froggy and listening to Connie singing 'Ave Maria'
in this strange swamp." How absurd an ending to life,
and yet, at the same time, considering what I'd been
through, how appropriate.

But after a long while, the sickening, dizzy feeling
began to subside and I managed to lift myself off the
floor. Using the line of student desks for support, I
slowly made it across the classroom to my own desk
and chair.

But now what? Here in my hour of need I had
left my cell phone in the car. The thought of the long,
painful journey out of the building and through the
palm court to the parking lot was far from pleasant,
so I worked at my computer until the sun began to

set. Then it was now or never, as God only knew what kind of creatures would come out of the darkness to do me in.

Using a large umbrella as a makeshift cane, I managed to hobble to the car and somehow drive home. Lying in bed, I finally got a good look at my injured foot. It resembled an eggplant! I prayed that God would work a miracle just for my benefit by Monday and the swelling would diminish along with the pain.

Though the Lord had temporarily forsaken me, the compassionate Mrs. Marian didn't, and, although my foot was a mangled mess and I was in pain for months, she made sure I received the best medical treatment. Clumping around in a leg cast for the next nine weeks, I fit right in with the elderly crowd at the local Publix.

"The baby Jesus statue shouldn't be placed in the nativity until Christmas Day," stated Mr. Cain passionately, referring to the stone display placed in front of the entrance to the school.

"We're not open on Christmas Day, so no one would see it then," was Mrs. Marian's more practical response. While this heated debate on proper manger protocol raged in the back of the office, another drama unfolded in the front. Just as a prospective family was getting a sales pitch from the secretary, the kindergarten teacher came running in, towing a smirking little blond boy behind her.

"Call Brian's parents right away," she demanded. "He just took out his penis and showed it to the class!" That news transformed the shocked parents into a hard sell. Another tour the previous week ended when a palm frond fell in the courtyard and knocked the secretary flat to the ground in front of a touring family. Teachers or students screaming when they spotted a snake at their feet also served as a quick deterrent to new sign-ups.

The last school day before Christmas vacation consisted of parties in the classrooms followed by an early dismissal. The day began in the gym where a parent donated their month-old newborn to play the baby Jesus. Two sixth graders dressed as Joseph and Mary were kneeling in a wooden manger on the stage when some dramatic music began to blare away. When the rising stanzas reached a crescendo, the baby appeared between them after being pushed out from behind the curtain. It was met with cheers from the audience and wishful thinking by mothers- if childbirth could only be that easy!

At this dramatic moment, Mr. Cain, with all the fervor of a flagellant, began screaming manically, "Everyone step up, step up now and testify, testify to the baby Jesus!" With his wild urging, the students, many of whom had been out sick for the past week with colds and viruses and only came in today for their parties and gifts, lined up like lemmings to file past the baby and view it from a few germ-spreading inches away. Some middle-school students with smirks on their faces "testified" for the amusement of their friends, shouting into the microphone, "I love you baby Jesus." Then they rushed to their classrooms to stuff their faces and rip open their gifts that were provided by Secret Santa.

When I had the students make up their Christmas wish lists, all that appeared on it were gift cards. Maybe it was the combination of my 50s Christmas decorations and the fact that I'm old fashioned and that the students were only twelve years old, but I insisted on gifts that were tangible and wrapped. The presents were displayed under the classroom tree and opened one at a time while "Jingle Bell Rock" played in the background. Certain forms of celebration, performed for children as they were done in the past, are just more fun.

The class mother I had that year was a gem, and, due to her efforts, I was very well provided for that Christmas. Still limping from my fall, I mentioned this fact to a tough-talking teacher while we were carrying our gifts to the parking lot. "Well, you better hope that you don't get my class mother next year. Their family owns half of Narcissus, but she's a cheap bitch." The next year, this tough-talking prophecy, to my dismay, was fulfilled.

My damaged foot prevented me from returning home for Christmas that year and I was a little lonely. Yet my feeling of desolation would have been a lot worse but for the kindness of two of the teachers, who invited me over for Christmas Eve and Christmas Day, and, of all people, the lady working at the local dry cleaners, who could always make me laugh.

Nancy was also from the northeast and not too far from my age, so we shared the same sphere of reference. If no one else were in the store, we made fun of the other customers' sometimes awful clothing. For Halloween, she dressed as a black cat in a skin-tight outfit and complained that the long tail kept getting in the way. She bragged that other male customers, upon seeing her in the cat costume, lingered long and told her that she gave them a woody. Her outrageous behavior was the perfect antidote for loneliness. So during the vacation I always found some article of clothing that needed cleaning.

In addition to the strange dry cleaner was the even more peculiar dental office. Two weeks after being in Florida, I developed a terrible toothache and was referred by another teacher to a local dentist. As my cavity was being filled by the dentist, his female assistant sensually rubbed my hand and shoulder.

Stupidly, I just thought that perhaps this was how dental treatments were performed in Florida, but when I mentioned it to the amused teachers the next day, they advised me otherwise.

I would need those laughs to get me through the school year, as after the Christmas vacation things went from bad to worse. The arrogant attitude of some of the wealthy, entitled, spoiled brat students combined with the total lack of support, or even communication, from Mr. Cain in dealing with behavior problems was a lethal combination that could only lead to trouble.

To add to my misery, the people living upstairs from me in the gated condo complex partied all night, playing loud music and dragging furniture across the floor. This nightmare of noise had somehow become a repeating theme in my life. There were mornings I went into the school shaking from lack of sleep. A few times I showered at three in the morning, drove to the school, and slept in the parking lot. I called the cops twice, then made up my mind to move when my lease was up. What a wonderful welcome to Florida.

Boom, boom, boom came the heavy tread on the floorboards in the hallway of the building my classroom was in, announcing the presence of the ponderous, holier-than-thou teacher who only came into this building to use the copy machine. Her departure always found the machine either out of paper or, worse, broken. But this time, she stopped at my open door on her march to the copy room.

"I was just in the office and Mrs. Marian said she would like to see you," came the shouted words from a large mouth coated with clown-like red lipstick. Then Miss Halo continued toward her daily mission of mechanical destruction.

Mrs. Marian, a concerned expression on her normally placid face, was seated at her desk and bade me to sit at the chair facing her. Mr. Cain hovered over me.

"Sharon and Grace were in here earlier and handed me this list of their classmates who they said cheated on your last test," Mrs. Marian informed me, pushing a piece of paper across the desk toward me. I quickly scanned the list of nine names written in Sharon's barely legible handwriting. But why would they rat out their fellow classmates and risk being ostracized?

Reading this question in my puzzled expression, Mrs. Marian said, "Sharon and Grace had studied hard for the test and were angry that the others didn't but received better grades. And they had me promise not to tell that I acquired this information from them." Then she proceeded to tell me how the cheaters had gotten the answers from a student who had taken, and obviously kept, the test from last year.

So, what to do? Occasionally I had caught a student cheating and had given them a zero on the test. But this involved almost half the class. Plus, some of the cheaters were on, or being considered for, the National Honor Society.

Mr. Cain, in his usual wimpy way, tried to evade the whole situation and, worse still, shift the blame for it to me.

"Well, they just saw temptation and took it," he offered as a lame excuse for the students' behavior. "And did you give them the same test they were given last year?" he asked me pointedly.

"I gave them the test that came with the course curriculum," I replied. Then I couldn't help throwing in, "I didn't teach them last year, so I don't know what test they were given. And though I put a Latin phase on the board every morning before class, I certainly never wrote 'MUNDUS VULT DECIPI, ERGO DECIPIATUR.'"

Apparently, Mr. Cain had forgotten he had been their teacher, and the fact that I pointed it out left him chagrined.

Mrs. Marian was quick to recover the uncomfortable situation and, surprisingly, came up with a firm solution.

"Give everyone that cheated on that test fifty for a grade. Any of the students in the Honor Society who cheated will be put out of it, and any students being considered will not be elected to it," she decreed, the corners of her mouth curved down and an eyebrow raised in grim determination, like a Judith poised over a Holofernes.

And so it was done. The parents were notified and, though some vehemently protested that she dare discipline their darlings, Mrs. Marian, unlike the wimpy Mr. Cain, stood firm. Yet the students chastised were not the least bit sorry they cheated, only very, very sorry that they had been caught.

As in most elementary schools, the younger students can be more enthusiastic and enjoyable then the ones suffering through the early stages of puberty. Viewing with delight the 1950s Florida display set up in my classroom, the shorter students from the fourth grade, whose classroom was in the room next to mine, had trouble seeing items on the upper shelf, so I put them on one of the desks. The cheap bottle of "Orange Blossom Perfume," with its glued-on white paper flower, caught the interest of some of the girls, so I took it out of the orange box that had been its home for the past half century.

"Would any of you like to try some to see what it smells like?" I asked. That was a dumb question, because the entire group, including the boys, wanted a daub on their arms.

Suddenly, like an invisible creature in a 1950s low-budget monster movie, the sickeningly sweet smell took over the room, seeming to permeate into every desk and chair and devouring all available oxygen molecules. I quickly sent the kids back to their homeroom. Upon their entrance, Miss Lee, the fourth-grade teacher, who was a lovely and helpful young lady, flung her hand to her throat, started coughing, and quickly began opening windows. I confessed to her what I had done and retreated from the noisy confusion to the relative safety of my room.

A moment later, all sound suddenly ceased, and my first anguished thought was, "I've killed them, I've killed all those sweet students with poisonous, cheap, old souvenir perfume." Then my thoughts turned practical as I could picture myself in headlines as the perpetrator of this freak accident, and I wondered if I would go to jail for my stupidity. I raced back to their room and was greatly relieved to find the smell dissipating and the students quietly working at their desks. Miss Lee looked at me, shaking her finger in a burlesque of a naughty gesture and, smiling, signaling that the bad boy was forgiven.

But it was hard to forgive, or even comprehend, some of the torturous rituals the totally out-of-touch-with-reality religious fanatics running the school put the students and teachers through. The day for the "Living Rosary," performed outside under a pitiless sun by the students, was one of the worst. It was May. This is Florida. Put those two together and you have a heat index that Satan would envy. Disregarding everybody's discomfort, the students, in full uniforms, were formed in a rosary circle, and the decades began.

In the blinding, glaring heat, it wasn't long before some of the "beads" began to faint. They were unceremoniously hauled away into the air conditioned building closest to where they collapsed. I had positioned myself in the small amount of shade that was near the doorway, my fear of the snakes in the nearby shrubbery overshadowed by my throbbing temples and clinging, soaked-with-sweat shirt. When I spotted Mr. Cain going throughout the spectators, asking the teachers he spotted to fill in for the vacant beads, I quickly ducked into the building and hid out in the boys' room, figuring that if I got caught I could use the excuse that I had to "go."

After an extended period, I ventured back outside just in time for the wrap-up with the sign of the cross. Spotting some of the teachers standing in the rosary, with their faces beet red and their bodies drenched in perspiration, I felt no qualm of conscience, only a feeling of vast relief that I had made my escape.

The wealthy town of Narcissus, whose inhabitants lounged dreaming (and drinking) behind the high walls of their bougainvillea-scented gated communities, was known for its millionaire "sugar daddies" and calculating women seeking their companionship and many, many monies. The class trip that first year consisted of a tour of a museum and then lunch in a nice restaurant. I was seated at a table with four attractive young mothers, their bodies trim and toned from buff personal trainers, their straight hair bleached blond and parted to the side - with seemed to be *de rigueur* in Narcissus - and every inch of them pumped and polished.

We were seated near the front door and the students had their own tables far across the room in the back, so no one would have known we were with them. Upon entering the restaurant and seeing the four pretty young women seated with a man old enough to be their father, each upscale patron cast smirking, assuming glances in our direction. The look in their eyes showed that, in their opinion, I was a pig that needed a harem to make me happy, and that I must possess millions for procurement (and possibly a hidden attribute not put in a bill-fold). I was immensely flattered.

Chapter 16

Saved or Sizzled

"We ought to be able to get rid of a teacher next year," was the ominous vow of one of the more obnoxious seventh-grade boys to his classmates upon hearing that their two barely manageable classes would be combined into one big horror show the next year. They still bragged about getting a teacher fired while they were in the first grade by pushing her past the point of human endurance. When she lashed out she was quickly let go by Mrs. Marian and, to the delight of her tormentors, went weeping to the parking lot and departed for good.

So, the year that they were together as one large, mean-spirited class was an unmitigated nightmare for the teachers. Their behavior seemed to be based on a barometer of money measurement. The more money that their family had, the more odious they were. You would think that if you had millions and lived in a mansion you would sit back, smile, and be kind and generous to all. But in many instances, especially with this group, such was not the case.

What didn't help, and in fact caused most of the problems, was Mr. Cain's complete lack of disciplining skills. Despite all his Bible reading, he must have sneezed through the proverb "For these commands are a lamp, this teaching is a light, and the corrections of discipline are the way to life." For some reason, he wanted to be a hero to the students, and his undermining of the teachers' authority and playing the game of "Good Cop / Bad Cop," coupled with no consequences for misbehavior, caused unbelievable problems and resentment. For me, it led to an ending that wasn't exactly the sweet scene out of *Goodbye, Mr. Chips.*

No matter how much you love teaching, and no matter how proficient you are at it, in the end, you can only teach if the students will let you. They have to at least meet you halfway, but this horrid group wouldn't give an inch and were only concerned with their own nonsense, not with the acquisition of even a minimum amount of knowledge. Only when they wanted a favor did their behavior soften and they became almost human for a minute of two. Once they got what they wanted, they returned to their rude ways in a split second.

Noticing that this barbarian behavior was accomplished with impunity, many of the sixth and seventh graders decided to join in the fun. Pantsing became a popular pastime, especially during gym days when unbelted shorts could quickly be pulled down to the ankles.

Either out of curiosity or pure perversity, the sixth-grade girls decided to get a good look at the inside of the boys' bathroom, and at the boys who were unzipped and in there. Screaming and laughing, they pushed the door open and stormed in. The boys ran out past them into the hall, zipping up while on route. When informed of the bathroom raid by a disgusted teacher, Mr. Cain's response was his usual mode of operation - another prayer.

"When you get to high school, boys are going to try to make you do things that you don't want to do," warned the pretty tenth-grade girl standing next to Mr. Cain at the morning assembly, and I wondered what the hell this was all about.

"You have to learn how to say no to them and keep your self-dignity," she went on, haltingly and somewhat embarrassed. The teachers with younger students began to rapidly depart with their classes in tow. When the girl continued in the same vein, I decided to quickly decamp with my homeroom students.

"What was she talking about?" asked Julie, a very innocent student who still believed in Santa Claus and the Easter Bunny.

"I really have no idea," I answered honestly, but, burning with curiosity, I made a silent vow to find out as soon as possible, and I knew just who to ask.

The moment my first prep began, I raced to the religion teacher's room and was relieved to find her alone at her desk, correcting papers. I entered uninvited and closed the door quickly behind me.

"What was that all about this morning?"

"Mr. Cain's an idiot," she spit out furiously. "That girl used to go to this school and now goes to the Catholic high school in Narcissus. She was caught having sex with a boy in the hallway and was going to get kicked out, but her parents are going to pay to add a new wing onto the school and Mr. Cain wanted her penance to be warning to the girls at this school not to do what she did," she said in one quick sentence, leaving me with two impressions. Once again, throwing a large amount of money at a problem sometimes solves it. And, from a detached, practical viewpoint, why didn't the girl and her ardent beau just sneak outside and have their tryst behind a palm tree or in a car? And as for a penance, wouldn't a few Rosaries have sufficed, rather than this "scarlet letter" treatment?

As if dealing with all this nonsense wasn't trying enough, the year had an abnormal amount of "momsters," mothers who believed everything that their kids (always the trouble makers) tell them and whose sole purpose in life is to complain about everything the teachers do. They never have the decency to take their grievances directly to a teacher, regardless of how approachable that teacher may be. Being two-faced and back-stabbing seem second nature to them, and they take great satisfaction in making a teacher's life barely worth living.

The worst woman of this genre was, unfortunately, my class mother. On the wrong side of forty, she still dressed like a sixteen-year-old and came into the school between her Botox sessions smiling, wiggling, and giggling. I soon learned that her niceness was as phony as her breast implants.

Because she was my class mother, I gave her son a starring role in the several theater productions that I did at the school, though he possessed very limited talent. But it was her other son in the eighth grade who was an arrogant cuss and was constantly disrupting the class. When I finally gave him a demerit and had him write a letter of apology to me, she silently declared total war. Though still smiling sweetly whenever our paths crossed, she constantly camped out in Mr. Cain's office and whined about imaginary injustices I perpetrated against her darlings.

Guerrilla warfare was also being carried out against me by a witch-like mafia mom from New Jersey (no parent at the school was born in Florida) who was, by any measure, a certified nut case. She once bragged to me that, as a student, she tore the veil off a nun and got kicked out of school, and her impulsive, vicious nature hadn't dissipated at all in adulthood. Her heavyweight daughter was in my homeroom and constantly causing trouble. If I dared to reprimand her for any wrongdoing, she somehow managed to get word to Machine Gun Mom in a minute, probably via a cleverly concealed cellphone. Her mom would then dash to the school, double park her broomstick out front, and burst into the office to badmouth me.

I was always waiting for her to do a New Jersey table flip (or desk flip) while in a rage in my classroom, or at least take her shoe off and throw it at my head as my aunts used to do if I aggravated them when I was a kid. And it wouldn't have surprised me to find a dead fish in my office box. It never reached that point, but the damage she did with her lies and big mouth was worse than any physical damage she may have inflicted.

"I had to perform four funerals last week. I am so sick of consoling people. When I retire, I'm getting a cabin in the woods and I don't want to see anyone ever again," whispered a smiling Father Bob to me as we stood in the warm sunshine of the courtyard just before the Mass started. Although he said this in a jovial tone, I knew that he meant it. Decades earlier, he had been a bartender in his decadent youth and, in a way, he was still serving alcohol with the intent of making people feel better about themselves. He knew how to joke around and entertain, and I much preferred when he performed a Mass than the dreadfully boring, dried-up, old fossil that was his companion priest.

"Did you see the news that Mother Angelica died?" he questioned me, laughing. Mother Angelica was an ancient nun who had appeared on a Catholic TV channel since the dawn of creation and recited endless Rosaries. "She must have been two hundred years old," he continued in a jesting tone. Then the younger students started singing while the older students stayed trapped in their daydreams, signaling the Mass was beginning.

"Oh well, show time. There are children to indoctrinate and sins to punish," he moaned and, putting on an invisible pious priest mask, started parading devoutly to the altar. I seated myself with my homeroom, hoping I wouldn't have to move any of their seats due to bad behavior.

That same afternoon, Mr. Cain showed just how severe his dislike was for me. I had made the suggestion at an earlier meeting that it would be a good idea if misbehaving students were made to write an apology letter to the teacher they had disrespected. The other teachers backed me up, Mrs. Marion agreed, and Mr. Cain had reluctantly concurred.

The obnoxious son of my devious class mother wouldn't stop talking during class the previous day, so I issued him a demerit and he was supposed to write me an apology letter and present it to Mr. Cain. As I passed through the office on my way to the meeting, I saw a paper in my box. On it was scribbled a weak, at best, sort of apology.

"I'm sorry I screwed around in your class today – Jamie," was the extent of the insincere endeavor. It must have taken a whole ten seconds to compose and was far from my idea of an apology letter.

"Are there any problems with discipline?" questioned Mrs. Marian during the meeting. Still having the paper with me, I spoke out, reading the letter and saying that it was far from my idea of an apology. Mrs. Marian agreed and told Mr. Cain to have Jamie write me a real letter. Then the meeting ended and the teachers flew out the door as fast as birds when the cage door is left open, and for the same reason.

I raced out along with them and had just seated myself at my desk to shut down my computer when Mr. Cain came into the room with his fists clenched and exploded.

"I didn't appreciate that at all. This is the second time you've done this to me!" he screamed, blood vessels suddenly standing out starkly on his neck and forehead. And then, before I could even gather my thoughts to respond, he stormed out, giving proof for the billionth time in history to the proverb that "anger rests in the bosom of fools."

Munching on a cookie I had grabbed on my way out of the meeting, I leaned back in my chair and tried to make some sense of the stupid scene I had just witnessed. The fact that Mr. Cain despised me was clear enough, possibly for unintentionally displaying the glaring fact that he was doing such a pitiful job as school disciplinarian. But he mentioned that this was the second time I did "this," and I didn't remember a first time. For some reason, he was harboring a deep resentment over a perceived trespass against him, and this scene set the stage for the sad events that were soon to arrive. If he had said, "Thou shall see me at Philippi," Mr. Cain's tone could not have been more ominous, and I knew that if there was any way he could, he would send my career at the school rapidly spiraling toward the drain.

That chance came only too soon. Mrs. Marian announced that she was leaving the school, the job of headmaster was up for grabs, and Mr. Cain was the first to enter the ring. Although his chances seemed slim at first, much maneuvering behind the scenes by the cult still holding sway over the school eliminated the more qualified candidates one by one, as ruthlessly as the Israelites destroying the towns in Canaan. And so it came to pass that he achieved the exalted position, much to the chagrin of the many teachers who previously had to put up with his ineptitude and wondered what this change would bring.

I knew that none of my comrades would believe me when I told them that my head would soon be demanded on a silver platter. It didn't take long either. For someone normally so wishy-washy and vacillating, Mr. Cain suddenly moved with the speed of a bullet.

He assumed the heavenly throne on May 1st and on the afternoon of May 2nd, as I was showing the students the movie *The Good Earth*, I was summoned over the PA system to appear in his office at the end of the day.

"The theme of the story is that, sadly, many times people aren't really appreciated until they are gone," I said to the class after watching the tear-jerking ending, when the long suffering and self-sacrificing

O-lan dies an Academy Award-winning death. In retrospect, the timing of that statement on that particular day would be the height of irony.

The announcement from the office filled me with a sense of foreboding. It was like feeling a cold finger on my shoulder or hearing the wail of a banshee, as I had heard this same summons once before, in another place and time.

"We are moving in another direction (whatever the hell that meant) and are not renewing your contract for next year. You can resign if you want," Mr. Cain nervously blurted out to me in front of the school accountant he had forced to be there as an embarrassed witness. "Thank you for all you have done for us."

If I hadn't been so thoroughly disgusted with the place at this point I would have made some sort of protest, but my only words were coldly practical.

"I would hope that you will be paying me to the end of my contract?" My question was rhetorical, as we still had a month of classes, the final exams, and the graduation left to go.

"Of course, and thanks for taking this so well," he responded, visibly relieved that he hadn't had to deal with any drama. I guess he expected me to either scream, curse, cry, or faint at the news, and hence the need for another human in the room to either calm me down as I raged around the room or catch me before I hit the ground in a swoon. All I did was sit there in a strange detachment, thinking how ironic it was that the person who caused my problems at the school should be the one to, in a twisted way, release me from them.

Pulling out of the parking lot, I glanced up at the school sign that had just been changed for an event the next week. "We Appreciate Our Teachers" it read, and the irony wasn't lost on me. For obvious reasons, I felt far from appreciated after sacrificing all my spare time for the past two years of my life helping my students in any way possible and promoting the school to outside organizations. Now I was thrown away like a piece of trash. I made a silent vow to myself never to teach again.

That last month at the school was tough, to say the least. I had decided not to tell the parents or students until after the final exams, though I did inform the teachers and office staff, who were shocked. I took no joy in saying "I told you so," nor would I let Mr. Cain off the hook by resigning. I had nothing to be embarrassed about as I had done nothing wrong, so why should I resign? Let him deal with the parents when they got the news.

I could have fought for the job by appearing before the Board, but why bother? I had taught their kids for the past two years and all they did was praise me. And now this! Even as a child I couldn't understand why people wanted to live in a certain neighborhood or join a certain club if the people there were adamant about not wanting them. Why would you want to be with those people anyway? And that was exactly how I felt now.

Also, the novelty of witnessing and being a part of the lifestyle of the wealthy, complete with galas where they would shake their chic, expensive booties on the dance floor, golf outings, and cocktails by the pool had worn off a year ago. Troubles are universal, and their money didn't make them immune from the same problems as the parents of my students in the ghetto, disease and divorce being the most prevalent. Although the Narcissus crowd had the money for better doctors and lawyers, the pain, anxiety, and effect on their children were the same. Of course, there were some wonderful students I would miss, but I consoled myself with the fact that, eventually, being a teacher, they would all leave me soon anyway. And when they left, they would change into strangers I would no longer know.

The day after the exams were over, I told the parents and the sixth and seventh-grade students that I wasn't asked back for the next year and I would miss them very much.

Many of the parents complained heatedly about my removal, but the Lord had hardened Pharaoh Cain's heart and he would not listen. One mother, when I informed her of my dismissal, said she was going to pass out and had to lean on a palm tree for support. I was very flattered, even though the fact that she was still recovering from surgery may have had something to do with her sudden weakness of the knees. But I had made much of a fuss over her shy son and she appreciated it.

Then came the graduation. The tradition at the Garden of Eden School was for the middle-school teachers to wear graduation gowns and, after the Mass ended, sit on the stage facing the parents and students while the diplomas were given out. My responses to the Mass were as perfunctory as the students', as witnessing the hypocrisy at this school had stripped me of much of my faith, leaving me hanging onto what was left by my fingernails. My prayers at bedtime, the same ones since childhood, being my only sincere solace and devotion.

Seated upon the stage with the other teachers afforded a panoramic view of everyone in the gym, and I looked about with distaste. I had seen this scenario before, but where? Then it came to me in a flash: the scene from the movie *Carrie* that had scared me so much decades earlier that I was afraid to go home in the dark and had to sleep at a friend's house. My sinful friend and her boyfriend slept in the bedroom and I was relegated to the living room couch. When I awoke screaming from a nightmare, I went to the bedroom to inform them that it was only a nightmare and I was fine. But the room lay deserted and, after a short search, I found its former occupants terrified and hiding in the attic.

"We thought someone came in and was killing you," they explained as a reason for their flight. My heroes! Obviously, if I was being attacked neither of them would have come to my rescue. And, as my eyes swept the audience in front of me, neither had any of them.

In the gym scene in *Carrie*, Sissy Spacek is crowned prom queen on the stage, only to have a bucket of pig's blood dumped on her head by her cruel classmates. Using her telekinetic powers, she has the doors to the gym slam shut, the fire hoses come off the walls and spray the crowd, and the whole place burst into flames like a modern version of Sodom and Gomorrah.

I sat on the stage, lost in a childlike fantasy of having those same powers now to release on this scorpion's nest. I would forgo the fire part or anything that would cause real physical harm, but the fire hose part would work well. My eyes lighted on my class mother seated in the fourth row and, smirking, I pictured the full fury of a hose trained on her, her recently Brazilian butt-lifted ass flying through the air across the gym. The silly vision somehow made enduring this awful evening suddenly worthwhile.

The final nonsense that night was provided by
Mr. Cain who, holding up a cross to the audience,
explained that the vertical part of the cross
represented God's love for us and the horizontal
attachment represented the love of a man for his wife.
That bizarre interpretation could be taken with many
sexual connotations, the nicest being the missionary
position, and then going rapidly downhill from there.

That speech on wife love concluded the ceremony,
and I had no intention of staying for the dinner part
to "break bread" with the eighth-grade families. I
walked out the door of the gym as unobserved as a
ghost. Then I passed through the campus and the
parking lot, still clad in the graduation hat and gown.
Not bothering to take the gown off, I drove home in
the same outfit, hoping I wouldn't be involved in an
accident and have to explain my strange attire.

The next day, I drove back to the school to return
the garment and take the remaining items out of my
classroom. When I went out the front gate for the last
time, who was entering, of all people, but Mrs. Mafia
and her little lunatic daughter. Although I could have
said anything I wanted to them at this point with
nothing to lose, I just wished them a good vacation,
thinking that, with all the misery of the past two
years, how fitting that they should be my last memory
of the school.

Yet as a counter balance to students and parents
like them, there were the incredibly kind families I

encountered over the years. I had always decorated my classroom with toys and items that corresponded with the time periods that were being taught. One sixth-grade boy, James, had a great imagination, an attribute so lacking in many students today. He seemed to be fascinated with the vintage artifacts as kids don't see many toys anymore, only electronic devices. When I commenced the arduous task of cleaning out my classroom, I would ask him if he wanted this or that item. He always said yes and seemed to take a genuine joy in them. When I told his class that I was leaving, he presented me with a letter the next day, and I read it later with eyes that clouded over, for the last time, with tears. Somehow, this simple note from "the world according to James" balanced all the bad memories of my teaching career and suddenly made it worth all the annoyance that went along with it. Worth more!

Dear Mr. Consorte,

Thank you for giving me and my friends all of those toys. It really means something to me because you're the only teacher I've had that gives us toys. You are an amazing teacher and thank you for being so nice.

Love, James

It is always hard to have the things you love in life suddenly taken away from you. As you get older, it becomes more and more difficult to replace them, then finally impossible. I refuse to risk a broken heart again. But I'm happy that I will always have the memories of the many students like James, and I dedicate this book to them and the many hardworking teachers and administrators in the Catholic school system who are kind and considerate but, because of those attributes, don't always make good copy.

Printed in the USA
CPSIA information can be obtained
at www.ICGtesting.com
LVHW011624240224
772733LV00001B/193